THE MAN FROM THE STAKED PLAINS

Young Gade Haggard rode south in search of adventure but ended up fighting a war during which he saw his brothers hang for desertion. The man who gave the fateful order was a cavalry major called Reuben Flack — the very man who had married Gade's widowed mother. And now Flack is on his trail. So, too, is the enigmatic gunman Diamond Jack Sloane. Can Gade survive the inevitable showdown? Will justice be done? Only Judge Colt will decide.

Books by Jack Sheriff
in the Linford Western Library:

BURY HIM DEEP, IN TOMBSTONE

JACK SHERIFF

◆

THE MAN
FROM THE
STAKED PLAINS

Complete and Unabridged

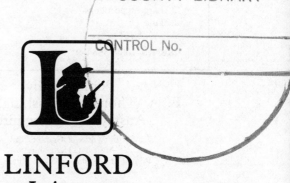

LINFORD
Leicester

First published in Great Britain in 1998 by
Robert Hale Limited
London

First Linford Edition
published 1999
by arrangement with
Robert Hale Limited
London

British Library CIP Data

Sheriff, Jack
    The man from the staked plains.
    —Large print ed.—
    Linford western library
    1. Western stories
    2. Large type books
    I. Title
    823.9'14 [F]

    ISBN 0–7089–5564–9

Published by
F. A. Thorpe (Publishing) Ltd.
Anstey, Leicestershire

Set by Words & Graphics Ltd.
Anstey, Leicestershire
Printed and bound in Great Britain by
T. J. International Ltd., Padstow, Cornwall

This book is printed on acid-free paper

Part One

The Gathering

1

With the arrival of spring it was his habit to step outside the old cabin when the sun was still a cold light beyond the horizon. After a night swathed in rough blankets he relished the feel of the chill breeze on his bare chest, the wash of clear, pine-scented air through lungs that were clogged and stale after hours of sleep in the single, shuttered room; the intensity of the light, after dreaming restlessly of haunting shadows.

The cabin was set on a grassy, tree-lined bluff to the south of the long slopes leading to higher ground, and movement of any kind was rare. In the silence of those early mornings he would wash at the wooden bucket outside the door, and the splash of icy water, the snort of his own breathing as he sluiced his face, the rasp of the razor — all of these simple sounds were as startling as a twig cracking in silent woodland.

None of this had made him careless. Each morning he would ease himself from his warm bed, pad across the dusty boards to the door and set his grey eyes carefully searching the trail that cut across the rolling plains towards the town of Desolation.

Occasionally he would see the outlines of a Studebaker wagon, crawling across the landscape towards San Angelo, some twenty-five miles to the north. Late one afternoon he had sat and watched a medium-sized herd of longhorns being driven west, and had wondered idly if the trail boss was about to risk the ninety-mile trip across the Staked Plains blazed by Joe Loving, aiming for Castle Gap, the swift-running waters of the Pecos and the long trail north.

And for a time his thoughts went with that rolling dust cloud, lost in nostalgia, for beyond Castle Gap and the Pecos lay Comanche Springs, and the cool green pastures of his home.

In his careful, daily scrutiny of the Texas plains watered by the three Concho rivers, he had seen nothing to suggest that the ruthless man who was hunting him had picked up the scent. Yet each time he took that first step over the threshold, fear tightened his stomach muscles, had done so every day for six months.

Inevitably, although he still took care, his morning ritual had become a habit. With the passing of time the eyes that carefully scanned the arrow-straight trail saw that, and that alone. And the man who finally broke his solitude came like a ghost in the night, and with infinite patience became a part of the landscape.

'Mornin', Gade.'

Shattering the silence, the sound of his own name was a physical blow that rocked him back on his heels. He sucked in his breath, felt the hairs on his neck prickle; thought of the .45 in its holster, the leather belt shiny with shells hanging yards away on the back of the broken chair.

'Always said you were part Injun, Shako,' he said. 'You been sat there all night?'

The chuckle was low and hoarse. Tight in against the trees on a ragged pinto that seemed carved from stone, Shako Gunn was all knobs and angles wrapped in an old Indian blanket. The greasy brim of his battered hat drooped over lank grey hair. Black eyes glittered. The seamed face was of tanned leather, cracking with age.

'Most of it. Like to froze clear through. I still could've blowed you back inside, Gade, with half your backbone missing.' The black eyes shifted and Gade Haggard saw that the gloved claws of Shako Gunn's hands clutched a battered shotgun, the barrel resting rock steady across the pommel.

'Yeah,' Haggard said, letting his breath go. 'But even a sonofabitch like you wouldn't ride all this way to kill the only friend he ever had.'

'Friend? Now, there's a word I ain't heard in a while,' Gunn said. He kicked his left leg forward and up over the horse's neck and slid easily from the saddle, trailed the blanket down the short slope to the cabin, stood spread-legged in front of Gade Haggard.

'You invitin' me in?'

For a long moment Gade Haggard stood there, a tall, bone-thin man with muscles like rope, grey eyes staring bleakly from a gaunt face framed by long dark hair, elbows bent, the thumbs of his big hands hooked into the waistband of washed-out pants.

Then he turned and led the way wordlessly into the cabin.

The smell of Shako Gunn was all about him as he moved, pungent, part earth, part animal. Haggard watched the gaunt figure drift past and pad across the bare boards on soft moccasins, rest the shotgun against the bunk then take the steaming pot off the stove, pour hot black coffee into two mugs.

'To old times,' Gunn grated. His black eyes were alive, hungry. He lifted a mug, drank deep, and as Gade Haggard slipped into his worn shirt and tucked it into his pants he realized, with enormous relief, that the lonely days of uncertainty and watching lay in the past.

'Old times are forgotten times,' he said softly, feeding Gunn the lie, inviting the response.

'By you?' Shako Gunn laughed harshly, handed Haggard a mug. 'Your own father hanged your brothers, Gade, held you at gunpoint to watch 'em swing.'

'Your gun, Sergeant,' Haggard said. 'I was backed up against a wagon, your Army Colt under my chin.' He sipped the scalding coffee too fast, felt the tears spring to his eyes, blinked, said, 'You never took your eyes off me. When those troopers used their quirts, drove both broncs squealing from under my helpless kin, you felt me flinch, watched my eyes.'

'Saw 'em there,' Shako Gunn said, and now his own voice was hushed, his eyes distant. 'Two reflections. Dark shadows, twistin' and swingin across the moon.'

'You could've stopped it.'

'Me?' Gunn cocked an eyebrow, dragged the grey blanket across his shoulders, clasped his gloved hands about the hot mug.

'We were all in it,' Haggard said. 'Grant, Dougie . . . me, you.'

'Desertion made better sense than servin' under Reuben Flack. But in that clear moonlight they caught us cold. Dougie and Grant went too soon, too fast, Gade. They was through the trees and halfway across to the Yankee lines when our outlyin' piquets spotted 'em. No way I could cover. Best I could do was swear to your pa you was with me, wanted no part of it.'

'My stepfather. And he didn't believe you.'

'No.' Shako Gunn drained the coffee,

carefully set the empty mug on the table, stared speculatively across at Gade Haggard.

'No,' he said again, 'Major Flack, he sure didn't believe me. He knew wherever your brothers went, you went. But he listened to me tellin' him the lie, and he took your brothers and lashed their hands with rawhide and put the ropes around their necks and then, before he gave the word, he looked at you.'

'And I kept my mouth shut.'

'No man wants to hang,' Shako Gunn said flatly. 'But because of what you did, when the war ended you came here 'stead of goin' home. And because by killing your brothers Flack also broke your ma's heart, you'll ride with me to Desolation.'

Haggard stirred. 'He's that close?'

'Bin there a week. Took a room over the saloon.' Gunn let the information sink in, saw the frown, said softly, 'And in case you're wonderin' why he's here, there's a ranch way out west of town just been bought by a man named Mil Ransome, rode with Custer at Gettysburg . . . '

He caught the sudden interest in Haggard's eyes, nodded. 'A Yankee with a slice of Texas. But worse than that, he's got himself a pretty Texan wife, gal with hair like ripe corn. Your sister, Libbie. Waited till your ma had recovered some from losin' three sons in the war — two of 'em permanent — then left home with her blessing.'

Gade Haggard swore softly. 'The war's a year gone. When's he goin' to quit chasin' Yankees?'

'Not till the day he dies.'

'And now Libbie's involved. Flack's had his eye on that girl from the day he rode out'f the Plains. He took Ma for his wife, but his body lusted after younger flesh — an' a goddamn Yankee's pushed his nose clear out of joint . . . '

Gade Haggard dragged a hand across his face, heard the rasp of whiskers, thought he heard another

11

sound, outside, the faintest clink of metal on stone.

He remembered then that Shako Gunn had stepped down off his bronc and interrupted a morning routine that had become a ritual; had called his name before his eyes had time to focus on that distant trail.

And he knew that had been a bad mistake. Shako Gunn was here because of Major Reuben Flack, the tall, fanatical Texan who, fifteen years ago, had appeared like a grey ghost out of the blistering heat of the Staked Plains. He'd slaked his thirst at the Pecos, then ridden on to the Haggard spread beyond Comanche Springs, and with a fetching grin that masked a heart of stone, had stepped down from his weary mount and swept a grieving young widow off her feet.

'I was fourteen, Dougie and Grant a couple of years younger,' Gade Haggard said softly. 'I should have killed him then, when he was too weak to lift an iron.'

12

He looked up, met the eyes of the old friend who had been alongside him through the last two long years of a savage war; caught in them the sudden flicker of warning; saw the mouth open to yell —

Glass shattered behind him. A slug thunked into the cabin's back wall. A second drew sparks from the iron stove. A third plucked at his hair as he dived for the dirt floor.

Then he rolled. He grabbed for his gunbelt, brought the rickety chair clattering down. The Army Colt spilled from the oiled holster. Haggard snatched at the smooth butt, cocked the hammer. Like a snake he wriggled towards the open door.

'No!'

He rolled onto his back, sixgun held high, melted into the shadows. 'Must've trailed me, stayed back of those tall trees,' Gunn hissed. 'Couldn't've seen you step outside. Would've took you then, single aimed shot.'

'Flack's men?'

'Sure. For six months I've been a thorn under their saddles, the itch they can't scratch.'

He slipped past Haggard, said, 'Stay out of sight.' Then roared, 'Hold your fire, I'm a-comin' out!' and stepped down onto the stone step.

Haggard wriggled back across the cabin. He stopped when he was beyond the rectangle of morning light flooding through the door, hitched himself into a sitting position against the bunk. From there he watched Shako Gunn walk thirty yards down the slope to meet the two riders who emerged from the trees and approached the cabin.

'Part Injun, part Irish,' Haggard muttered, face bleak. 'You need both, old friend — or we're both dead.'

Shako Gunn stopped. He stood side on, his left shoulder towards the riders. The grey blanket hung from his bony shoulders. The shotgun was cocked, the barrel resting in the crook of his left arm.

The gunmen drew rein. The leaner

of the two had the face of a hawk and carried a Spencer breechloader, butt on his thigh, muzzle pointing skywards. He leaned to one side to peer past Gunn.

'Haggard ain't there,' Gunn said.

The second man was a stocky Mexican armed with twin Remingtons in tied-down holsters. He wore a huge, ragged sombrero. Under his sweeping moustache his mouth was twisted in a cynical sneer.

'Only your word for that,' he stated, and spat into the dust.

'Well now,' Shako Gunn said softly. And suddenly the morning crackled with menace.

'Step aside, old man,' said the lean gunman.

'He's got a shotgun,' the Mexican said. 'He thinks a shotgun makes him immortal.'

'No,' Shako Gunn said. 'What this shotgun does is make *you* think.'

'Sure. What I'm thinkin' is, you mebbe get one of us, then you're dead,' said the man with the Spencer. He cocked the hammer, let the rifle swing almost lazily to cover Gunn.

Shako Gunn laughed. 'Blast away, friend. But while you're squeezin' that Spencer's trigger, this shotgun'll cut one of you fellers off at waist level.'

'Two men die,' said the Mexican with amusement, 'for an empty god-damn cabin.'

'You called me a liar,' Shako Gunn said. 'When the smoke clears, one of you'll know for sure my word was good.' He grinned. 'But right now, I ain't sayin' which one.'

From the shadows inside the cabin Gade Haggard heard the creak of leather as the lean gunman shifted in the saddle; caught the brief exchange of glances; noted the immobility of Shako Gunn, and knew from experience that the lined face would be blank, the black eyes infinitely patient.

Then it was over. The lean man swore, jerked his head, and the two riders wheeled their mounts and rode away from the cabin at a steady lope.

Gunn watched them go, then walked up the hill to the edge of the trees. He picked up the trailing reins and led his horse across the grass to the cabin.

With his back to the open door he slid the shotgun into its saddle scabbard. Out of the corner of his mouth he said, 'You remember Sam Pickens?'

'I remember,' Haggard said. He climbed off the floor, sat on the edge of the bunk, eased his stiff legs.

'Sure you do,' Gunn said. 'And that's one more reason you'll ride to Desolation.'

He swung into the saddle, dragged the blanket around his shoulders. Then without a backward glance he kicked the pinto in the ribs and set off towards the ribbon of trail over which the dust stirred up by Flack's gunmen still drifted.

2

The lean man dressed from head to foot in black was unnaturally still, had been so for many long minutes. He sat in a hard, straight-backed chair in the corner of the room, watching Reuben Flack.

Flack was tall, powerfully built, a man in his early fifties with a hard face and long, grey-blond hair. He wore the non-regulation short jacket of a Confederate cavalry major, a star glittering at each side of the high collar, the wide lapels buttoned back to show the faded yellow lining. Blue trousers with a yellow stripe were tucked into scuffed, high-top knee-boots. His eyes blazed as he railed at the two surly gunmen.

The shabby room contained a sagging bed, four rickety chairs, a washstand with a cracked bowl, a round table covered by a torn cloth. Two worn saddle-bags lay on the bed's threadbare blankets. In the gathering gloom an oil lamp standing on the table cast its weak light on a whiskey bottle and two smeared glasses.

Behind Reuben Flack, drab net curtains wafted in the cool evening breeze. From time to time, when Flack paused for breath, the clink of bottle against glass could be heard from the saloon directly below. But that was all. No hoarse guffaws rattled the windows. No women squealed shrilly. No swing doors clattered as drunken waddies stumbled out into the dusty street.

The overall silence was disturbing, oppressive. Yet none of this had any effect on the watching figure.

Several times, as Reuben Flack ripped into the two gunmen with a volley of lurid curses, the man's thin lips twisted in what might have been a smile, and the lamplight caught the gleam of white teeth. His legs were outstretched, ankles crossed. The only parts of him not in shadow were the black, shiny boots. Once, when Flack moved to the table, tilted the oil lamp to light his fat cigar from the hot chimney, the shaft of light caught the scarred butt of the man's jutting sixgun.

And always, from the deepest shadows, there was the eerie, sinister glitter of his single eye.

With a final bellow of frustrated rage, Flack dismissed the gunmen. The door crashed shut. Footsteps thundered down the stairs.

'Oh, goddamn them. Damn them to hell,' Reuben Flack gritted.

'Wrong,' said the man in the corner.

Flack swivelled, glaring.

'How so?'

'You want a man to come to you, make it look easy.'

'Ames and Diaz were trailing Shako Gunn, he led them to Gade Haggard's cabin. I want Haggard dead. But they let that crafty sonofabitch turn his shotgun on them, then were too scared to call his bluff.'

'Bluff?' The man in black uncrossed his ankles. A gloved hand moved to a shirt pocket, extracted a slender, black cheroot. 'Only Gunn knows the truth of that — but he watched Ames and Diaz back down, and he'll have taken note.'

Reuben Flack watched the man in black lazily uncoil from the chair, step into the lamplight, bend to light the cheroot from the hot lamp then turn and stretch to his full height. He was as thin as a whip. The gunbelt carrying the Dragoon Colt hung heavy on bony hips. Over his left eye-socket a black patch was held in place by a thin silk ribbon. High cheek-bones jutted over sunken cheeks. The mouth was a slash. His one, glittering black eye was alight with amusement.

'So now,' Flack mused, 'as Haggard and Gunn see it there's nothing stoppin' them from ridin' in, settlin' old scores?'

The man in black nodded, his dark eye amused. 'Sure. And that's their mistake. I'll take care of Haggard for you, but have you considered how the girl'll feel when she knows you're behind her brother's death?'

'I'll worry about that.' Flack laughed harshly. 'Let me tell you about Gade Haggard. First time I saw him, he was a skinny kid bossin' a spread for his widowed ma. Took one look at me with those sharp grey eyes, forked the nearest bronc and headed south. Saw no more of him until a year after Fort Sumter when he rode into my camp to join the rebels. Twenty-five or six by then, rawhide tough, used a name he'd been given by the bandits he rode with after the war with Mexico. Word is in that conflict he sided with Santa Anna. When a man like that expresses loyalty to a cause, I tend to be somewhat cynical.'

'Renegade,' the man in black said, his voice bleak. 'Shortened to Gade by a kid six years old who thought him a hero. Same wide-eyed, innocent kid who got caught up in a gunfight in a

22

street in San Miguel. Took a slug in the chest, died alone and scared.' He drew on the cheroot, let blue smoke trickle from between thin lips. 'Gade Haggard fired the gun: the kid was my son.'

'The devil you say!' Reuben Flack breathed.

'His ma was a Mexican, the closest I got to having a woman of my own. She made my bed warm through a long winter, watched me ride out in the spring. Seems in the summer she gave birth in that same adobe shack, died of fever soon after. I never knew, never once set eyes on the boy. But by and by word reached me, and for the next few years if I had nothing else I had that knowledge inside me.'

'But Haggard took that away,' Reuben Flack said, a gleam in his eyes.

'And the war took Haggard where I couldn't follow. I bided my time, prayed he'd die hard, knew if he didn't I'd get to him somewhere, somehow.'

'That place is here; the time is now. I'm pleased I picked the right man.

A man not only fast with a gun, but carrying enough hate to kill.'

'I got hate enough for Gade Haggard, with plenty to spare,' the man in black said and, for an instant, the single eye blazed at the major, sending a sudden chill through Reuben Flack.

'Shako Gunn rode in not long after Ames and Diaz,' Flack said, frowning. He crossed to the bed, opened one of the saddle-bags, extracted a leather pouch the size of two clenched fists, tied with a draw-string. He hefted it, listened to the dull clink of metal, felt the considerable weight of the double eagles. 'You can brace Gunn downstairs in the bar,' he said. 'If I know Gade Haggard he'll ride in with the rising moon. With a long gun you could pick him off before he hits town.'

'No,' the man in black said flatly. 'A man dies by the gun, he needs to know why.' Again the eye fixed on Flack was alight with tightly contained fury.

'Suit yourself.' Reluctantly, Flack

handed him the weighty bag of gold coins, said, 'I'm not happy with cash up front . . . I'd feel a whole lot easier if . . . ' He waited, studied the gunman's impassive face, shrugged resignedly. 'You need me, you'll find me with Ames and Diaz at their camp on the loop in the river halfway to the Ransome spread — ten, fifteen miles west.' He pondered for a moment, said, 'If Haggard hears you've downed Gunn he'll come after you. That'll make it easy.'

'Never was likely to be hard,' the lean man said. He flicked the glowing cheroot towards the open window, stuffed the leather pouch inside his shirt, then crossed to the door and slipped out of the room like a silent black shadow.

For several moments, Reuben Flack stared at the closed door. Then he poured a measure of whiskey into one of the glasses, and with a flick of his thick wrist tossed the raw liquor down his throat. He gasped once, then chuckled harshly.

So, that was Jack Sloane. Arrogant. Mean. A cold-blooded killer who, under a variety of sobriquets, was feared throughout southern Texas: Black Jack, after his mode of dress; the Solitaire Kid, for his single eye; Diamond Jack, for his skill at shooting the centre pip from the ace of that name.

But surely that kind of sharpshooting wasn't needed. Shako Gunn was an ageing soldier, deadly with a shotgun but at a disadvantage against a fast-shooting gunslinger. Gade Haggard . . .

Flack frowned, pulled at his lip. An unknown. He'd told Jack Sloane that Haggard was rawhide tough, and that was true. He'd fought a good war. But that implied raw courage, not gunfighting skills, and little was known of his years riding with the border bandits.

Nevertheless, Flack mused, picking off Gade Haggard with a long gun made sense. Why take risks? Why adhere to some crazy, mythical gunfighter's code of fair play? Hell, his policy of ignoring that frontier bravado had seen him gun down more than one man from the shadows of a dark alley; seen him use his military authority to rid himself of enemies without danger to himself.

Flack strolled to the window, gazed down at the street where pools of lamplight washed over worn plank-walks; frowned as he saw the man in black step down into the dust and saunter away in the direction of the livery stable.

What now? Diamond Jack Sloane had taken his gold — damn near broken the bank! — then ignored his advice and, by doing so, missed a clear chance to down Shako Gunn. He'd also said flatly that he wouldn't use the long rifle on Haggard, yet now he was heading for his horse.

Flack shook his head, turned away from the window. A strange man, with hidden depths. With hate to spare, or so he said; and for an instant Flack allowed himself a measure of pity for the man who was next on the gunman's list.

Then he shrugged dismissively. Hell, no matter. How Sloane did the job, where he went when it was done, was his affair. And he poured another stiff drink, raised the glass, his eyes distant.

That same policy of killing without scruples had also led him to hire Diamond Jack Sloane, who had walked in through that door and listened to the offer with an unholy light in his eye. Flack was quite capable of bushwhacking both Gunn and Haggard, but right now he was intent on dealing with the uppity blue belly who'd not only grabbed himself a whole chunk of Texas, but had taken the breathtakingly beautiful Libbie for his bride.

He'd lusted after that girl from the day he'd set eyes on her, Reuben Flack thought broodingly. Riding bareback, out past the corral, a thirteen year old with pigtails, blue eyes wide as she watched the arrival of the man from the Staked Plains.

The kid, Gade Haggard, had seen that encounter and, young as he was, he'd seen the look in Reuben Flack's eyes.

And that, Flack had long accepted, was just one more reason why Gade Haggard must die.

3

Held back in the thin stand of trees, the big roan moved restlessly. Metal jingled. Saddle leather creaked as Gade Haggard leaned forward, absently rubbing his gloved hand across the long mane.

His eyes were narrowed to thin slits as he gazed across a flat stretch of arid land, watching the plume of dust trailed by a horse moving fast away from Desolation. The horse was crossing his line of vision, heading due west towards where high clouds were still streaked red by the setting sun.

Any other time during the past six months, he would have paid the rider no heed, but the coming of Shako Gunn with news of Reuben Flack's arrival had altered his perceptions. He felt a pressing need to be suspicious of anything that moved, and had reined in half a mile from town, easing back under the trees to sniff the air like a lobo wolf.

From where Haggard watched, Desolation was a single, broad street of shabby commercial premises opening out into a sparse sprawl of tar-paper shacks and soddies. A trick of light washed the peeling slats of the general store's false front with the warm glow of evening, while touching the rusting iron roof of the saloon — across the street — with the cold light of the rising moon.

The racing horse had been led from the livery stable which lay across the street at an angle from the saloon and close to the edge of town. In the soft, hazy half-light, Haggard had watched the tall man in black swing into the saddle, had seen the flash of silvery light on metal as a long rifle had been held high then thrust into the saddle scabbard.

Sharps Buffalo, he'd figured. And

knowing that no more than 2,000 of those .45-.120 rifles had been manufactured, he'd sifted through memory, trying to match the gun with the lanky silhouette of the black-garbed rider.

Now, as the fast-moving horse diminished to a dark speck on the horizon, he grunted, dismissed the task as hopeless and turned his attention to hard facts.

Following the stand-off with the Flack's gunslingers, Shako Gunn had ridden away from the cabin without a backward glance. He would expect Haggard to find him. In a settlement the size of Desolation that wouldn't be difficult. But with Reuben Flack around, moving openly could be dangerous.

A match flared as Haggard lit a cigarette, the flame illuminating the face's deep hollows, glinting in grey eyes that were deep in thought.

After a deal of pondering during the ride down from the hills he had been forced to admit that Shako Gunn's actions had him stumped, both now and in the past.

Hell, the man had appeared out of nowhere in the middle of a war and become his shadow, always at his shoulder when the fighting was at its hottest, ramming a sixgun under his jaw to keep him silent when rash words would have got him hanged.

When the South was defeated they'd shared a last meal around a flickering campfire in the woods, then shaken hands and ridden their separate ways. But even then there had been something unfathomable lurking at the back of Gunn's steady dark eyes. Now, it appeared that for the past six months he had stuck like a leech to Reuben Flack's tail.

Why? Only reason Haggard could come up with was that Shako Gunn had looked out for him during the war and was doing the same now.

So, same question: why in hell would he do that?

Haggard shook his head, frowning

into the gathering gloom.

The general store across the street was owned by a fat, bearded man who'd once hunted buffalo for the railroads and lost his entire family to a Sioux war-party. Drunk most of the time now, he could, with difficulty, be roused, but once out of his bed he'd blunder about bellowing like a castrated bull, and was liable to attract the whole town.

That left the livery stables. Quiet now, and in darkness. Plenty of deep shadows filled with sweet hay where a man could rest easy and listen to the soft breathing of horses, the distant night sounds.

But still dangerous. He'd heard the place was manned by a crusty old ostler whose right eardrum had been shattered by Mex war cannons. When startled he was liable to reach for the old Hawken plains rifle he kept ready loaded, and blast anything that moved.

Which fact clearly made it safe

from casual prowlers, Haggard thought, grinning, and with sudden decision he flicked away the glowing cigarette and gently nudged his horse out into the clear moonlight.

It was but a short ride across the open ground to the edge of town. Haggard let the roan take it at a walking pace, rocking easily with its motion, conscious of the daylight fading at his shoulder, the rising moon casting long shadows that turned the nearby alleys into dangerous passageways between buildings that were now no more than anonymous blocks of stark light and shade.

The town was worn out, dying from the flanks in, yet about it there hung an air of brooding menace. Gade Haggard sensed the cloying tension. The hairs on his neck prickled. He flexed his fingers, eased the Army Colt in its oiled holster as the horse carried him into the town on hooves muffled by dust, past the wide gallery of the general store, across the yawning entrance to the livery stable and into the deep shadows alongside the adjoining building.

Carefully, Haggard slid from the saddle, paused there, hand resting on the pommel. Across the street he could see through the swing doors into the dimly lit interior of a saloon that seemed as dead as the town. Directly above the batwings there was a window where lamplight gleamed behind thin net curtains.

As Haggard watched, a figure moved across the window, stood for a moment facing inwards. The lamplight outlined the bulk of the man, glinted on long blond hair, on the butt of an ivory-handled sixgun.

Haggard's breath hissed between his teeth. Without thought, his hand slid down smooth leather, came to rest on the cool stock of the Winchester. Eyes fixed on the window, he began to slide the rifle from the saddle boot.

Then the figure moved away. The chance, if he wanted it, had gone. And as he let the rifle slip back and the cold sweat burst from his brow, somewhere behind him a man chuckled drily.

'Your heart's not in it, Gade, or Reuben Flack'd be a dead man.'

Haggard swung around angrily, led the horse through the double doors into the stable, handed the reins to the old man who, with head canted to one side, limped crookedly from the office.

Then he followed the indistinct outline of Shako Gunn across to the nearest empty stall. Straw rustled beneath his feet. Dust and the pungent smell of manure stung his nostrils. In the gloom, he strained to make out the blanketed figure leaning against the plank partition.

'We haven't thought this through,' he said, then nodded swift understanding as Gunn raised a warning hand. 'This morning, you brought back old memories,' he went on, pitching his voice low, keeping the anger in check. 'At the time a natural fury muddied my thinking. A day's thought tells me I should confront Flack, look into the man's eyes, see what makes him tick.'

He listened to the ostler, busy with the horse, called, 'Loosen the cinch but leave the rig where it is, friend,' and again heard Gunn's laughter.

'He can't hear you too well,' he said, 'but if you carry on shouting like that you'll drag Ames and Diaz from the bar.'

'Let them come. They can take me to Flack.'

'You're crazy. You've been holed up in that shack too long, dreaming dreams.'

'Maybe. Those shadows haunt me, always. But we all knew the risk. In four years of war I saw deserters from both sides shot, hanged. Flack was going by the book, doing his duty.'

Shako Gunn stirred restlessly in the gloom. His eyes moved, watching Haggard, catching the light.

'A man who runs in peacetime ain't a deserter, my friend.'

The sudden silence was thicker than shadows. In it, Haggard sensed the fragile wall of justification he had painstakingly constructed around Reuben Flack begin to crumble. He moved aside as the ostler stomped past, reached out a hand to a timber upright, touched its strength for support.

'You mind explainin'?' he said huskily.

'Two days after your kin was hanged, we got word the war was over. But that was April sixteen, Gade.'

'You sayin' the war was already over when we ran for those Yankee lines? Flack hanged those boys a full seven days after Appomattox?'

'Sure. And knew what he was doin'. Kept his own private war goin', desperate to kill hisself a few more blue bellies.'

'And any loyal Johnny rebs sickened by his lust for blood,' Gade Haggard said bitterly.

'The blood lust's still there,' Shako Gunn said flatly — then broke off abruptly, melting into the shadows as spurs tinkled in the street and over by the office there was the oily click of a gun being cocked.

'Leave it be,' a harsh voice growled. A sixgun cracked, spurting flame. Sharp splinters of wood sang through the air.

The old ostler was a slight, crooked outline against the street lights. The blue steel of the Hawken plains rifle shifted, tilted harmlessly towards the luminous skies as he lowered the hammer.

He said, 'Knowed you was trouble, minute you rode in,' and spat wetly.

And as Haggard took a silent pace backwards, dropped his hand to his gun, there was sudden movement in the darkness behind him and hard metal rammed into his spine.

4

'Easy, feller.'

A boot replaced the gun in his back. A stiff leg thrust him violently towards the street. The ostler backed off, sharp eyes watchful. Beyond him, a lean figure stepped into the wide doorway, smoking sixgun still levelled.

'Haggard,' the man said, and there was suppressed fury in the thin tones.

Behind Haggard, the other man said, 'Where's your friend? Where's the old-timer in the blanket?'

'You came down from the hills, he followed you in,' Haggard said. 'Knowing Gunn, he's across the street proppin' up the bar.'

The ostler chuckled. 'Sure. Bin there all day.' Crinkled blue eyes flitted from one man to another, alighted on Haggard.

In the gloom, Gade Haggard thought

41

he detected the flutter of an eyelid, looked closer and to mask his sudden, shocked realization, said mildly, 'For a deaf man you sure don't miss much.'

'A busted eardrum don't affect a man's eyes,' the old man said. 'Been watchin' these two, and the other feller with the long yaller hair, fancy pistols.' He moved away, boots brushing through straw to where a flimsy ladder rose to a dark opening in the loft floor. 'Now looks like I've got a mite more watchin' to do . . . '

'Move.' The sharp command cut through the old man's ramblings as the lean man in the doorway waggled the sixgun. Ames, Haggard guessed, stepping towards the street. The man behind him with the ready boot and the Mex accent would be Diaz.

'No need for gunplay,' he said. 'I rode to town looking for Flack.'

'So now you've found him,' the Mexican said. He laughed harshly. A match was flicked by a thumbnail. Blue smoke drifted, bringing with it the reek of a strong cheroot.

Then they were out in the open, crossing towards the saloon, the two gunmen flanking Haggard. They brushed past the three horses, dozing hip-shot at the rail; mounted the steps, the rickety boardwalk sagging under their weight.

Again Diaz lifted his boot, sending the swing doors crashing open. They trooped into a long, ill-lit room where a crude plank bar rested on empty oak barrels, tables stood bare and unoccupied on the sawdust-strewn floor, and the aproned bartender's moist eyes followed, without interest, their progress towards the steep stairs.

At the top, Ames turned and led the way to the room at the front of the building. Following close behind him, Haggard felt his heartbeat quicken.

He thought about the contradictions in the town of Desolation. The deaf ostler who appeared bent and frail but carried a long rifle and had sharp eyes. The old soldier who wrapped himself in a frayed Indian blanket but spat his contempt at hired gunslingers. A tall man in black, riding into the night with a Sharps Buffalo . . . '

Ames motioned him forwards and Haggard went past into a small room lit by a single oil lamp standing on a rough table. Also on the table was a glittering sixgun, an engraved, ivory-handled .45 Colt Peacemaker, one of a matched pair that Haggard knew well.

A gloved hand was at rest alongside the sixgun. The gun's muzzle pointed directly at Haggard's belt buckle.

He came to a halt, stood relaxed, hands loose at his sides. As if at a great distance he was aware of Ames holstering the sixgun and moving to the window, of Diaz remaining behind him at the door.

Then he grinned sardonically, lifted his gaze, looked straight into the cruel, steel-blue eyes of Reuben Flack and knew he had been wrong to fabricate excuses for this man's deeds.

'So you finally came a-lookin',' Haggard said.

Flack's laugh was a derisive bark. 'For you?' He shook his head, the blond, grey-streaked hair sweeping his shoulders. 'I stretched your brothers' necks before your eyes, watched what guts you had leak out your boots. You think I'd waste effort on you?'

'At dawn I was willing to give you the benefit of any doubt. Lookin' into your eyes now, I know you want me dead. I also know why, Flack. The lust for that young woman was burning in your eyes when you rode out of the Staked Plains. Well, I swear to God, before this is over you'll be back there, your body rotting under the blistering sun.'

'Talks good,' said the Mexican. 'You want I show him his mistake?'

'His mistake was comin' out of that shack,' Ames said, a sneer in his voice. 'Was hidin' in there all along, let an old man do his talkin'.'

Reuben Flack ignored them. His blue eyes, fixed on Haggard, now crinkled with amused derision. 'A year ago your

45

neck was saved because, in front of watching enlisted men, Shako Gunn spoke on your behalf.'

'Did the same today,' said Diaz. 'Looks like the old guy makes it his duty to protect this yeller-bellied *gringo*.'

'Maybe,' Flack said. 'But he ain't here now, so when you make your play, Haggard, you're on your own.'

'Boxed in, with nowhere to go,' Ames growled, and he shifted his weight expectantly, balancing on the balls of his feet.

The silence stretched painfully. Smoke from the Mexican's cheroot was a drifting pall caught by the heat of the yellow lamp. A floorboard creaked under Ames's weight. Reuben Flack's eyes were unwavering. His hand, alongside the fancy sixgun, was relaxed, fingers slightly curled.

And as Gade Haggard flicked his eyes in the direction of the window, somewhere high in the dark bulk that was the livery stable, he caught the glint of moonlight on metal, and he felt the sudden surge of excitement that came when in the midst of a battle the odds shifted in his favour.

'Old Gunn ain't here,' Haggard said, 'but his words still carry weight. Like him, I sure as hell aim to take one or more of you with me — and the way you're spaced, whoever's left standing when I go'll likely die in the crossfire.'

'Quit jawin',' Reuben Flack said flatly, 'and let's git this thing over.'

The wicked laugh bubbling from the lips of Diaz the Mexican was cut short as, with shocking suddenness, a heavy rifle boomed from across the street and the window shattered.

Ames gave vent to a roar of pain and anger as the hot slug plucked his sleeve and sliced the flesh of his upper arm. The same slug smashed into the lamp, extinguishing the flame. Coal oil and shards of glass sprayed the room.

In the sudden eerie half-light cast by the high moon, Reuben Flack reacted fast. The gloved hand moved three inches, slapped the butt of the sixgun. A forefinger curled around the trigger. The muzzle began to lift.

Behind Haggard, Diaz hissed through clenched teeth as flying glass slashed his cheek. Ames was a dark shape against the window. His right arm was bent, fingers curled over his .45. But he was slow, his draw hampered by pain and shock.

Oil hissed and smoked on the lamp's hot metal. Glass tinkled to the floor. And in that taut moment when time stood still, Gade Haggard took two fast steps and launched himself in a horizontal dive at Ames. His hard shoulder rammed into the lean gunman's soft underbelly, driving the air from his lungs. Haggard wrapped both arms around the gunman's middle, burying his head against the man's bow-taut body.

Somewhere in the room two sixguns blasted in rapid succession. But the shots were wild, both slugs drilling harmlessly into the thin timber walls.

The force of Haggard's dive slammed Ames off his feet. With a roar of shocked anger, the lean gunman was driven backwards. The backs of his thighs hit the low window sill. Arms flailing, he fell through the opening. His mouth gaped in a bellow of fear and pain as jagged slivers of glass jutting from the window frame sliced his shoulders and back.

Split seconds later the two men hit the plankwalk with a crunching thud. Ames took most of the weight. Haggard heard his explosive grunt as he rolled clear. Then he had pivoted on one foot and hand, using the impetus to bring him to his feet, hand slapping for his sixgun.

He had time only to realize that his holster was empty when Ames swung both legs in a sweeping arc and kicked his legs from under him. Haggard fell sideways. His shoulder hit the plankwalk with a bone-cracking thud. Instantly, his left arm went dead. Then, as Ames launched another scything kick, he rolled into the street to tumble beneath the hooves of the three tethered horses.

The startled animals reared back from the hitch rail, rawhide reins snapping taut. A stamping hoof cracked Haggard's ankle, sending a bolt of agony up his leg. He curled, rolled, came to his knees, flexed his numbed arm. Out of the corner of his eye, he saw Ames launch himself off the plankwalk. Then the gunman was on him, bony fists swinging.

A heavy punch slammed into Haggard's jaw. His head rocked. Light flared and his vision was fogged by a red mist. He fell back into the dust, spat blood, aimed a wild punch that grazed Ames's forehead. Then they were both rolling beneath the flashing hooves of the terrified horses, aiming wild, desperate punches, fists crashing brutally against the sharp bone of cheeks and jaw, sinking into soft flesh.

Above them, long manes tossing against the moon, the horses snorted in fright. Again the heavy rifle boomed. A voice roared. Distant footsteps hammered down wooden stairs.

Then Haggard was out from beneath the slashing hooves. With the crooked fingers of both hands he grasped the gunman's ripped shirt. He lurched backwards, used the gunman's weight to gain his feet, spun fast, slammed the lean figure against the hitchrail.

Ames's sweating face was streaked with dust and blood. His eyes blazed. His lips drew back from his teeth in a snarl as the peeled timber hitching pole dug into the small of his back. Spread-legged over him, Haggard swung a looping right to the gunman's jaw, followed it with a swinging left. Sweat and blood sprayed. Ames grunted as Haggard's fierce punches drove him backwards, body arched over the rail.

Then, head flung sideways as he spat out a tooth, Ames deliberately threw himself backwards. Using the hitch rail as a pivot, he slammed his bent knee up into Haggard's groin. Pain lanced like the thrust of hot steel into Haggard's belly. He groaned through clenched teeth. As he doubled up in agony he heard Ames's cruel laugh ring out. Then, still fighting the pain in his guts, he was straightened up by a vicious uppercut to the jaw. He staggered backwards, tripped, fell. A boot crashed against the side of the head.

Senses swimming, Haggard lay sprawled on his back with the taste of dust and blood in his mouth. Ames's dark bulk loomed over him, blotting out the light of the moon. Haggard lifted a knee, tried to raise himself on his elbows. Then he flopped back, braced his body to receive the stomping boots of the triumphant gunman.

Again the heavy rifle boomed. Dust spurted between Ames's spread feet. A cracked voice yelled, 'Next one blows yer belly through yer backbone!'

Ames crouched, twisted, slapped

leather. But his .45, too, had been lost in the fall. Hand empty he straightened slowly, turned to face the stable. And moving like a man whose reactions were slowed by too much hard liquor, Gade Haggard rolled clear, got his knees under him and climbed painfully to his feet.

Chest heaving as he gasped for breath, he shook his head to clear the red haze. He limped over to the sidewalk, located his Army Colt, stepped down between the restless horses and collected his battered hat from beneath their hooves. As he rammed it on his head he looked past the bloody, fuming Ames. In the dimness beyond the swing doors he saw moonlight glinting on blond hair, caught the red glow of a cheroot.

Diaz and Reuben Flack. Watching, waiting.

'Time to move on, Gade.'

Shako Gunn, calling from the livery. Haggard nodded thoughtfully, heard Ames growl, 'One day, feller, we'll git you when your friends're someplace else,' then turned and made for the stables.

As he stepped inside, Shako Gunn met him, leading his horse. Haggard took the reins, found a stirrup, swung himself into the saddle.

'Sam still got that Hawken pointed at Ames?'

'Until you're clear.'

'And you?'

'Flack let you walk away. Don't mean he'll do the same for me, but I guess I'll mosey over there anyway, wet my whistle, see if I kin figure what's makin' him tick.'

Haggard met the knowing gaze, nodded, said, 'It ain't over, you know that.'

Gunn laughed softly. 'Jest started, friend. Ride careful, now — and stay off the skyline.'

He slapped the horse's rump, stepped back, and with a swirl of the ragged blanket was gone.

Using his heels and tight reins,

Haggard wheeled the roan out into the street and kicked it into a fast gallop.

He flashed past Ames, standing helpless under the watchful gaze of old Sam Pickens and his Hawken; thought he saw a gloved hand wave mockingly from the doorway of the saloon.

Then he was out in the open, his horse pointed towards the one place he knew for sure Reuben Flack wouldn't come looking.

5

After the initial fast gallop away from Desolation, Diamond Jack Sloane eased back and rode steadily by the light of the moon. He let the big bay gelding pick its own way towards the foothills, only turning its head towards the north when he figured the somewhat half-hearted false trail he had laid had gone far enough.

An hour's riding brought him back onto the arrow-straight trail from Desolation, and he cast a fleeting glance towards the higher ground, seeing nothing in the deep shadows of the eastern slopes but knowing that up there lay the old trapper's cabin used by Gade Haggard.

One thought led to another, and Sloane found himself ruminating with some satisfaction on the lucky break that had brought him to Desolation on the trail of one man, and led him to another. He pulled off the trail and reined in for a while, smoked a leisurely cigarette in a cool glade. The shadows swallowed up his lean black figure. His eye was alert for movement along the back trail.

Not that he was expecting pursuit of any kind. Gade Haggard and the old-timer called Shako Gunn were as yet unaware of his presence in this part of Texas — if they knew of him at all.

Nevertheless, Diamond Jack knew that the deadly double game he was playing was fraught with danger, in particular from the flamboyant Confederate major who was only cognizant of half of a complicated tale.

Gade Haggard was almost certainly unaware that a young boy had died in a gunfight that was just one of many such skirmishes he had been involved in; even if he knew, it would be impossible for him to trace the boy's link with Diamond Jack.

But, long ago, Reuben Flack had abused a mere girl in a town in south Texas and it had almost cost him his life. He had fled north into the Llano Estacado — the Staked Plains — holed up in an isolated ridge of slabbed rock and, using his Winchester, had shot the horse out from under the grey-haired man who pursued him.

Then, in a fit of rage, he had used two slugs to smash the man's knees, and left him to die an agonizing death in the scorching heat.

The man whose bones lay bleached in the searing desert heat had been Frank Sloane, Diamond Jack's father. The young girl Reuben Flack had ravished — and who had subsequently died in the agony of a complicated birth — was Emma Sloane, Diamond Jack's fifteen-year-old sister.

No man easily forgets a brush with death. So it was likely that, with the desperate flight across the Staked Plains etched on his soul, the name of Emma

Sloane would burn forever in Reuben Flack's memory.

That being so, Diamond Jack thought, before too long he's going to make the connection and when he did, the loose ends of a tangled web that had been a heap of years in the spinning, would get themselves neatly tied, and Gade Haggard and Reuben Flack would get their just deserts.

Or, to put it in plain language, they'd die.

In the moonlight his grin was a cold and evil sight.

Reuben Flack had left two Sloanes dead or dying and ridden out of the Staked Plains to his first encounter with the young Gade Haggard.

Years later, by way of chance and a stray slug, Gade Haggard had shot dead Diamond Jack's son.

Twelve months after the War Between the States came to an end at Appomattox, a trail-weary Diamond Jack rode into Desolation to gun down Reuben Flack. He'd located him in the room over the saloon, climbed the stairs with murder glinting in his single eye, but been stopped cold when the hardeyed major took one look at the low-slung .44 Dragoon and told the shocked gunman he was looking for a shootist to kill a man called Gade Haggard.

'An' life sure don't get much queerer than that,' Diamond Jack Sloane said softly.

He tossed away the dead quirly and eased the bay back onto the trail. The night was clear. A warm breeze lifted the dust of his passing. He rode accompanied by the creak of saddle leather, the mournful cry of a coyote. Thirty minutes later he pushed up a gradual slope flanked by tall pines, crested the rise and looked out across a moonlit vista of flat grassland like a vast, shifting inland sea.

At this point the trail from Desolation became indistinct, kinked once, then ran arrow-straight for a thousand yards to the ranch that could be seen in the distance. The meandering

60

tributary of the Concho that irrigated the rich pastures was a silver ribbon running close to the dark cluster of ranch buildings. An L-shaped house was separated from the corral by a small garden and a hard-packed dirt yard. The long bunkhouse was tucked up against a tall barn. Pushed by the gentle breeze, the rotating vanes of a windmill reflected the moonlight, the thin creaking of the shaft carried like the cry of a cat on the night air.

Mil Ransome's place.

Mostly empty. Half-a-dozen horses, looked after by one old wrangler. A neglected spread recently taken over by a war-weary man hankering after land, much too soon for him to have bought in cattle or hired hands. A man enjoying the solitude of the plains with his young bride, knowing his temerity would have raised some hackles, but likely unaware of the hatred seething within Reuben Flack.

Diamond Jack Sloane had no time for north-south grievances, but if Mil

61

Ransome's marrying a fair-haired Texan had Flack foaming at the mouth, well, that was something Sloane could use. When the Texan wench also happened to be Gade Haggard's sister, the same pretty young girl who had caught Flack's lustful eye when he rode out of the Staked Plains and lingered like a stubborn virus in his blood ever since, it seemed to Jack Sloane that a quirk of fate had dealt him all four aces.

As he sat easy in the saddle, the night-scented pines dark at his back, the distant windows of the Ransome spread warm with the glow of oil lamps, Sloane knew that if he played those cards right, the hand he held was unbeatable.

Hell, wasn't even any call for him to push himself. In the still hour immediately preceding dawn, all men were vulnerable. A bleary-eyed Mil Ransome would put up scant resistance, and when the old wrangler took word to town that Diamond Jack Sloane had the Ransome woman, Reuben Flack and Gade Haggard would start paying their dues.

Oh, but he would see that it was a long and painful process, Sloane swore now, his single eye a vengeful slit as he gazed blindly into the night.

Their wickedness had caused him years of mental torture. In their turn they would sweat blood for endless days of a waking nightmare, his taunts haunting their imaginings as he kept one step ahead of them with the woman, holding them at bay with accurate fire from the Sharps Buffalo until he tired of the game, let them draw near — and killed them.

But before they died, he would kill the woman.

Sloane's gloved hands tugged the reins and he wheeled the horse away, pointed it across the grassy slope to the edge of the pines. It was but a few moments' work to unsaddle the bay and leave it to graze, to slip the thongs from his roll, spread his blankets against the bole of a tree and bed down for the night.

On the slopes above the Ransome spread, a contented Diamond Jack Sloane waited for the dawn.

6

'Leave it!'

Reuben Flack's words cracked out, freezing the Mexican as he dipped for his gun.

Behind the blanketed figure of Shako Gunn, the clacking of the swing doors slowed, stopped. At a flimsy table between the doors and the bar, Diaz settled back into his chair. Dark eyes narrowed against the curling smoke from his cheroot, he hissed his hatred, let his hand fall away from his studded holster.

Sitting forward, elbows on the table, hands idly toying with a greasy deck of cards, Reuben Flack laughed softly, called, 'You too, Ames. Sergeant Gunn, he can't hit a barn door with a rifle, but you'd best keep both hands in sight 'less you want that scattergun to take over where the Hawken left off.'

The man standing at the centre of the plank bar nursing his bruises tossed back his shot of whiskey and turned away in disgust.

As if to emphasize Flack's warning, the blued barrels of the shotgun resting on Gunn's left forearm swung lazily, sweeping across the room. Then the black eyes crinkled and a derisive smile curled the thin lips. He stepped away from the doors and his soft moccasins whispered across the dry boards as he padded to the bar. He took up a position at its roughsawn end, lay the shotgun flat on the liquor-stained timber, signalled to the sweating barman.

'Three of us,' Ames spat, glaring over his shoulder at Flack. 'We could've took him, easy.'

'There was two of you this morning,' Shako Gunn pointed out, 'an' you got took. I cain't see anyone here big enough to make much difference.'

The cards snapped as Flack riffled them irritably, slapped them on the table.

'You've been hangin' on my tail for six months, Gunn. Why?'

'Bidin' time,' Shako Gunn said. He picked up his glass, sent a silver coin ringing across the bar, lifted the glass to eye level, squinted at the liquid. 'Knew all along where Gade Haggard was hid up. Direction you was travellin', I figured you'd cut his trail 'fore too long.'

'So?'

Gunn drank, sucked his cheeks, sighed deeply. 'A man holed up alone for months on end loses his edge, gets lazy or careless. Knows what he wants to do, but maybe needs a prod so he's wide awake when the chance sneaks up on him.'

'Why you?'

'Remember Grace?'

'Haggard's ma?' Flack frowned. 'What the hell're you talkin' about, Gunn? I married the goddamn woman.'

'Married her, bedded her, then rode on out agin,' Shako Gunn said, nodding slowly, and something in his voice brought Ames's head around, eyes wary in the lean, bruised face.

'Why not?' Diaz said, grinning sardonically. 'I would do the same for any good-looking woman.'

'Yeah, but without no wedding bells,' Ames sneered.

'You lasted less than six months,' Shako Gunn said, his tone bleak, black eyes fixed on Flack. 'Rode out before dawn one day, that fine woman's life savings in your saddle-bag.'

'You talk too much,' Reuben Flack warned. He sat back, the unbuttoned cavalry jacket falling away from his fancy sixguns.

'It's a long, ugly story, an' needs tellin',' Gunn said. As if as an afterthought, he used the tip of his finger to swivel the shotgun on the bar so that the black holes of the twin muzzles pointed at the blond cavalryman.

'Three of us . . . ' Ames breathed again, eager now.

'Count Flack out,' Gunn said. 'The

man's sat all off balance, starin' down the barrel of a gun.'

'What I think, I think he's lookin' at the man who's been beddin' his wife,' Diaz said and, as the major's face suffused with sudden fury and his powerful left arm chopped backwards to smash into the Mexican's face and send him spilling from his chair, Shako Gunn's laughter was like the thin crackle of breaking ice.

'Nah,' he said derisively. 'One fine man gave her four kids, died of the fever, then a cheap womanizer rode out of the Staked Plains, ruined her life. I reckon Grace Haggard rightly decided enough was enough.'

'You denyin' you've bin there?' Flack demanded, his voice tight with fury. Pinned by the shotgun, hands flat on the table, his eyes shifted warily to watch the Mexican as he climbed off the floor.

'I came on the Haggard spread by chance,' Gunn said, 'ten years after you rode out, the war already a year old. With most of the hands away fightin', Grace and Libbie were two lonely, frightened women struggling to run a cattle ranch. Day I rode up they were in the empty bunkhouse, using an old muzzle-loader to fight off a band of Texan cut-throats figured the war as an excuse for robbery and murder.'

'That'd make it around April, '62,' Flack calculated, eyes narrowed. 'Same month Gade Haggard rode out of the woods on a beat-up mustang, enlisted in my outfit. Next day he was fighting at Shiloh.'

'An' Grant and Dougie got word of his arrival to Grace,' Gunn said, nodding. 'Laughin' through her tears when she rode from town with that letter, first she'd heard of her eldest boy in more'n eight long years . . . '

He broke off as Diaz swept his sombrero off the table, rammed it on his head and made for the bar. A trickle of blood ran down his unshaven chin. His hand trembled as he took the drink handed to him by the silent barman, tossed it back, grimaced as the stinging spirit bit into the badly split lip. He turned, hooked his elbows on the high bar, glowered at Reuben Flack.

'I stayed on as ramrod for twelve months,' Gunn told Flack. 'By then, Grace was out of her mind with worry. At her bidding I took off after Gade, caught up with him at Chancellorsville — and the rest you know.'

'But the war is over, *amigo*,' Diaz said, mumbling through his smashed lips. He had moved a little away from the bar and was leaning forward expectantly, arms hanging loose, fingers flexing as the anger fired by Reuben Flack's fierce blow turned on Shako Gunn. 'Ain't no reason for you to wet-nurse Gade Haggard, never was no reason for us to let you git away with it.'

As he spoke there was a sudden flurry of motion. Ames took a step back, then planted his hands on the bar and

71

vaulted over, stiff-arming the bartender to send him stumbling back against the laden shelves. Bottles crashed to the floor, shattered. The reek of raw whiskey rose to fill the room. Eyes fixed on Shako Gunn, Ames reached down beneath the bar, came up holding a sawn-off shotgun.

'This kinda evens things up,' he gloated, and his calloused thumb snicked back the twin hammers.

For long moments the room was silent, quivering with electric tension, men's nerves taut with the expectancy of violence, of bloodshed, of sudden death.

Then the major broke the deadlock.

'I told you,' Reuben Flack snapped at Ames. 'Put the gun up, back off, leave him be.'

'Hell, Flack . . . '

'Do it!'

Ames cursed softly, deliberated, then swung around furiously and slammed the shotgun against the startled barman's fat belly. Diaz straightened, rubbed sweating palms against his pants, shrugged the tension out of his shoulders. His puzzled black eyes flicked from Gunn to the relaxed Reuben Flack.

'Gettin' cold feet, Major?' Shako Gunn asked curiously.

'I hired a good man to do the job, rode in a couple of days ago with hate in his heart. Feller called Diamond Jack Sloane. Favours black, carries a big gun. Got more against Gade Haggard than I'll ever have.'

'But this man here is not Haggard,' Diaz argued. 'Why don't we kill him?'

Flack shrugged dismissively. 'Him and Haggard stick close as burrs to a cow's back. Sloane can finish the pair of them without raisin' a sweat.'

'Leaving your hands clean of Haggard's blood?' Shako Gunn shook his head in disbelief, picked up the shotgun, moved towards the doors.

Alongside Flack's table he paused, leaned down close, said, 'If Gade Haggard dies, Libbie'll need to be a mite slow-witted to believe you had nothing to do with it. If she swallows that, I still can't see any way you can explain killin' her new Yankee husband.'

'She's a Texan,' Flack said, his eyes blazing with patriotic fire.

'Sure,' Gunn said happily, 'an' that says it all. You kill her man, she'll tear your goddamn eyes out.'

'Oh, this I must see,' Diaz whispered fervently.

'Stick with Flack, it might get interestin',' Shako Gunn advised with a grin. 'Hell, lettin' Gade Haggard ride out keeps your hands clean,' he told Flack, 'but it sure gives him time to warn Mil Ransome and his pretty Texan wife. I hate to tell you your business, Major, but you're playin' this all wrong.'

As Gunn delivered his parting shot, swung on his heel with a swirl of the ragged blanket and pushed open the swing doors, it seemed that Reuben Flack was lost for words. Then his face lightened, and a cruel grin creased his florid countenance.

'You're forgetting Diamond Jack Sloane,' he called. 'Before the night's out, Gade Haggard'll be dead meat out on the prairie. He'll have no breath to give warnings — and, come breakfast, I'll ride to the Ransome spread and Libbie Haggard'll be reachin' for her widow's rags.'

★ ★ ★

Diamond Jack Sloane's wide swing across the flat country lying between the Concho rivers, intended to mislead pursuers, was a considerable waste of time. When Gade Haggard headed for the cabin that had been his home for six months, his eyes were fixed firmly on the distant foothills but his mind was elsewhere, deep in thought.

Strangely, there was no room in those thoughts for the dark stranger with the Sharps Buffalo who had ridden off into the night. But maybe that was to be expected. When he rode out of Desolation, Gade Haggard was a confused man.

He'd fought in two savage wars in the space of twelve years and had more tactical savvy and plain common sense than most men. Yet, despite the blunt warnings from Shako Gunn, he had drifted into a tense confrontation with Reuben Flack when the odds against him were stacked high. By the time Sam Pickens cut loose with his Hawken plains rifle, he was staring death in the face. Thanks to the old ostler's covering fire, he escaped with little more than a few bruises and a bad case of dented pride.

Well, bruises had never bothered him too much, and the damage to his pride should jolt him out of the lethargy caused by six months of feeling sorry for himself.

But why had Reuben Flack held back?

As he lay helpless in the dust after the brawl with Ames, Flack could have

76

killed him with a single bullet. Instead, he watched, waited, and held his fire — and it was this that had Haggard scratching his head.

Or maybe there was a simple explanation. Pickens was past sixty and was deaf enough — or play-acted convincingly enough — to seem dim-witted. But during the war his recklessness and raw courage had been legendary. Flack would have remembered this, for Pickens had fought under him all the way from Bull Run to Appomattox.

Gade Haggard laughed softly, eased his horse back to a slow walk as he built a cigarette, contentedly watched the smoke drift in the moonlight as he relaxed in the saddle.

Hell, he hadn't recognized the ostler as an old army *compadre*, not at first. Shako Gunn had dropped the hint that morning, and Haggard knew the man who ran Desolation's stables was deaf. But he hadn't made the connection until Pickens winked at him and he'd seen through the ragged growth of beard, the long hair, and realized that this was the man who, the horse soldiers swore, could shoot the stars out of the night sky given a long enough rifle.

Assuming, that was, that he got through the long day's fighting without his recklessness getting him killed.

Haggard flicked the glowing ash, his eyes pensive.

When he rolled out of bed that morning, he had been a man alone, haunted by memories, living with an unnatural fear of one man and his burning hatred. Now, all that had changed. In the wily Shako Gunn and the veteran Sam Pickens he had companions tough as whang-leather. The arrival of the Yankee rancher, Mil Ransome, seemed to have diverted Flack's hatred. And because the sister he hadn't seen since she was a scrawny fourteen year old was in danger, Haggard was forced to rise above his fear.

After months of waiting, it was time for action.

Thoughtfully, he pinched the cigarette, nudged the roan with his heels, built up the pace to an easy canter which he maintained for another mile before turning off the trail into the deeper shadows lying in the folds beneath the tree-lined high ground.

The urgency was in him to ride straight to the Ransome spread, break the bad news, then offer his help. But common sense told him that Reuben Flack had no reason to make his move before dawn. Unaware that a fanatical Texan patriot was gunning for him, Mil Ransome was going nowhere.

And Flack, well, he was a vainglorious man who would make a deliberate choice to ride in with the sun rising at his back, seeing himself as a golden figure atop a fine horse, out to defend the sanctity of the South and the State of Texas. Cavalry pennants fluttering in the breeze, flanked by two loyal soldiers, he would approach the

Ransome spread knowing that right was on his side; ready, if necessary, to die for his cause.

But this was in Flack's mind. The reality, the truth, was more tawdry.

Ames and Diaz were scum from the dusty border towns of Texas, men who had sacked the town of Lawrence with Quantrill and now lived by the gun. The cause they would murder for was nothing grander than the handful of double eagles that would soon jingle in their pockets. That money would be put there by Reuben Flack.

No pennants would fly on the ride from Desolation. The uniform Flack wore would be stained and torn, the badges of rank without authority, the noble cause the weak excuse of a cold-blooded killer, the dawn chosen not for its fresh, clean sunlight but for its ability to bring the spirits of the strongest of men to their lowest ebb.

Gade Haggard was familiar with the dawn.

Gradually, the stand of pines grew in

size until it stood out black and ragged against the night skies. As he drew nearer the cabin became discernible to Haggard, cold and silent, but a comforting sight. He dismounted wearily, unsaddled, fed and watered his horse and let it run free in the pole corral tucked in beneath the trees.

The meal he cooked that night was simple, but hot and nourishing, the coffee strong and black. When he rolled into his blankets, he was a long time staring at the paler rectangle of the window, his mind too restless to sleep.

But it was a welcome restlessness. For the first time in months, Gade Haggard was looking forward with excitement to the start of a new day.

Part Two

The Abduction

7

'Rider coming, Mil.'

The girl's voice rang out clear and sweet, her warm breath misting white in the crisp air. Standing straight and slim in a light cotton shirt, split riding skirt and tooled leather boots, Libbie Ransome had blonde hair tied back with a red ribbon and level grey eyes that she and her brother Gade had inherited from their mother.

'Must be lost,' Mil Ransome remarked. 'Ain't no trail through here.' He was crossing the yard from the barn, a compact, dark man wearing faded denim work clothes and a battered blue army hat. He was carrying a small axe. Over in the corral, Walt Coburn, the bow-legged old wrangler who was the only one to stay on when the spread changed hands, was squinting under his raised hand into the sun, jaws working on a wad of tobacco.

'Or looking for work,' Libbie said, strolling out of the garden to meet her husband. 'Didn't you leave word at the livery with Sam Pickens we'd be needing hands?'

'Yeah, but he knows there's no hurry. Better remind him when you get to town.'

He moved alongside her, rested his hand for a moment on the firm warmth of her shoulder, said, 'I'll see what he wants,' and walked away from the house towards where two dusty cottonwoods drooped their branches over a plank seat.

'Coffee's still hot, plenty of it,' Libbie called after him, and Ransome nodded, glanced across to the corral to check on Coburn, then turned to meet the stranger.

* * *

Diamond Jack Sloane had rolled out of his blankets at first light, breakfasted

86

on cold jerky washed down with water from his canteen, then hunkered down on the crest of the rise to scan the Ransome spread through field-glasses.

The pale rays of the rising sun painted the ranch buildings a thin gold. Mist from the river lay like a soft, waist-high white blanket across the rich grassland. In the motionless air, the windmill's blades were still, its shaft silent.

First signs of movement came from the bunkhouse. A wiry old man emerged, coughed, stretched, then bent to splash his face with water from a wooden bucket. Ablutions finished, he bit off a hunk of chewing tobacco, scratched himself and wandered across to the corral.

'One,' Jack Sloane murmured.

He was a cautious man who took few risks, and overnight he had decided against making his move too early. Weighing up the danger of Mil Ransome having a couple of good men on his payroll against the threat of Reuben

Flack riding in with the sun at his back seemed like a fine balancing act. But Sloane figured that if he took a chance and jumped without looking, he could wind up dead.

He had patience, he had nerves of iron. Lady Luck had delivered Reuben Flack and Gade Haggard to him on a plate. He had waited too long to risk losing them both for the sake of thirty minutes' eye-scouting. In the event, it took no longer than that for him to know for sure that the old man spitting tobacco juice into the dust was the sum total of Mil Ransome's corrida.

Fifteen minutes after the old man emerged, a young woman came out of the house, engaged him in a conversation that seemed to be about a fine dun gelding watching them from the corral. While they were talking, a dark-haired man appeared, hitched his pants, said something to the others in passing. Faint laughter drifted to Sloane's sharp ears as the dark man swung open the barn doors and went inside.

Sloane kept the glasses on the ranch for a further fifteen minutes. Satisfied with his assessment, he took his time saddling the bay, checked the loads and well-oiled actions of his big Dragoon and the Sharps Buffalo, then mounted up and pointed the horse down the slope.

He sensed they'd spotted him long before he neared the yard, had expected it and was unconcerned. The old wrangler had saddled the dun gelding and was leading it out of the corral. Now he stopped. The woman was watching the dark man who had moved away from the house and was standing near the two cottonwoods, one hand hanging loose, the other holding the small axe at his side as he awaited Sloane's arrival.

No gun, Sloane noted. Mil Ransome, unarmed — or near as damnit. One old man. And the woman, Libbie.

The bay carried him close to Ransome.

Sloane reined in, eased his weight in the saddle then settled back. As a fickle breeze twitched the black silk ribbon securing his patch he let his keen eye roam carelessly over the yard, the buildings; deliberately let his gaze linger insolently on the woman until a faint flush coloured her cheeks and she turned away.

'You're Mil Ransome,' he said softly to the man. 'The Yankee.' Then he waited, saw the frown, the slow burn of anger.

'If you're a traveller, passing through, you're welcome to refreshment,' Ransome said curtly. 'Otherwise, I'd advise you to ride on.'

Sloane chuckled wickedly. 'Not without the woman,' he said.

Suddenly, Mil Ransome's eyes were empty, jaw muscles bunched in a face carved from stone. Almost absently, he brought up the axe, knuckles gleaming white on the haft, rested the heavy head in the palm of his other hand.

'What do you want?'

'Two men, dead,' Sloane said laconically. 'Reuben Flack, Gade Haggard.' Without taking his eyes off the rancher he heard the woman gasp.

'That's not what you said.'

'No. What I said was, I ain't leavin' without the woman,' Sloane repeated.

Ransome frowned. 'You're not making sense.'

'But you're wasting time. Yes or no, Ransome? Easy, or hard?'

His world collapsing about him, Mil Ransome let the words hang in the air; a question with only one possible answer; an answer that would cost him his life. Then, with a crooked smile, a half turn of his head, he called loudly, clearly, 'Libbie, run for the house.'

Diamond Jack Sloane saw the woman's head jerk as if struck, saw her mouth open, her eyes widen, sensed rather than heard the old wrangler's hissing intake of breath.

Then Sloane drew the heavy Dragoon Colt and shot Mil Ransome twice in the chest.

The twin blasts shattered the morning peace. Heavy slugs slammed into the rancher, drove him backwards. Blood blossomed wetly on the denim shirt. He took two wobbly steps. Then the strength leaked out of his muscles and his legs buckled. He hit the ground on his back, flopped, one arm flung wide. The axe flew high, bounced once, rang musically against stone.

For an instant there was a deathly hush. Then the woman screamed. Almost at once the scream died in her throat. She took a slow, stumbling pace towards the inert figure of her husband. Her face was chalk white, her eyes enormous. One hand pushed feebly, as if warding off the cold killer. The other lifted to her mouth, knuckles jammed against her teeth as she moaned.

The old wrangler, still clinging to the dun's reins, spat out his plug and roared a warning. 'Move, Libbie! This way, girl, now!'

With amusement, Sloane watched her falter. Hatred, terror, disgust, sadness, all those emotions flickered across her white face, were reflected in her huge eyes. Then she took a deep, ragged breath. With a final horrified glance at the man lying in a glistening pool of blood she turned and, in a frenzied dash, sprinted thirty feet to meet the old wrangler. She tore the dun's reins from his hand; found a swinging stirrup with the second clumsy try and flung herself into the saddle. In the same, instinctive movement, she spun the horse and raked its ribs with her heels.

Responding instantly it leaped forward, reached a full gallop in four tremendous, lunging strides. Libbie Ransome lay flat along the horse's neck, strained face buried in the flowing mane, hands fiercely gripping the reins close to the bit.

Sloane thought she would ride him down. Then the wild-eyed, snorting dun brushed past and was gone, hooves rattling a kettledrum rhythm across the yard then changing to a muffled pounding as it turned on to the overgrown trail.

'Well, now,' Diamond Jack said.

He stepped down from the big bay, slid the Sharps from the saddle boot, threw a swift, warning glance at the wrangler. Unhurriedly, he stepped over the dead man and went around the wooden seat. There he dropped to one knee, rested the Sharps on the seat's backrest, eased back the hammer; bent his head to snug the flat of the stock against his cheek, peered along the sights.

'Leave her be, you sonofabitch!

'Just the horse, old-timer. The girl's got a job to do.' Sloane chuckled. 'An' seein' as she's going to need a fresh mount, throw a saddle on that frisky paint pony.'

The dun was eating up the ground, already halfway along the thousand-yard straight. The kink in the trail Sloane had noticed from the rise was marked by thickets of mesquite. Ignoring the racing dun he inched his body sideways, carrying the stock with him so that the barrel of the Sharps swung the opposite way to line up on the edge of the thick scrub.

The early morning mist was thinning. What was left hung motionless.

The fickle breeze had died. There was no wind.

And now the fast-moving horse was approaching the bend in the trail, its hoofbeats a whisper of sound.

Again Diamond Jack snugged down against the stock. He felt his heartbeat quicken. His black-gloved finger slipped inside the trigger guard. He slowed his breathing; willed the tension out of his muscles; watched the distant brown shape change course, veer to the right, present its side to the deadly chunk of flying lead that would be delivered by the buffalo gun.

Sloane squeezed the trigger.

The explosion was thunderous. Flame belched from the octagonal barrel. The hard walnut stock kicked savagely against Sloane's shoulder.

95

'Missed her, you bastard!' Walt Coburn cried gleefully.

Sloane snorted with contempt. He stood up, walked towards the bay.

As he did so it seemed to the wrangler, gazing anxiously at the outline of the distant thickets, that the ground itself was jerked from beneath the dun's flying hooves. Still running, the horse went down in a crumpled heap, slid, lay still. Dust spouted, hung in a thin cloud. The woman was a rag doll, arms flapping helplessly as she tumbled into the mesquite.

Then Diamond Jack Sloane was in the saddle. He leaned forward to ram the still-smoking Sharps into the boot, wheeled the bay towards Walt Coburn and touched it with his heels. At his approach the wrangler, face greasy with sweat and twisted with despair and loathing, backed hastily away from the saddled paint.

Another, raw emotion was visible, one the old man fought valiantly to mask behind a fierce glare, an instinctive bracing of bony shoulders. But he was wasting his time. Diamond Jack had seen naked fear many times, and if it affected him at all it merely gave him a moment of fleeting amusement.

As the old man continued to back off, Sloane gathered the paint's reins. Watching the retreating figure with a gaze that now showed complete indifference, he transferred the reins to his left hand. Then he drew the Dragoon and shot Walt Coburn in the centre of his lined forehead.

Sloane watched just long enough to register the hit, the ugly black hole, the shower of bright blood. He didn't linger to see the old man fall. Leading the spirited little paint pony, he rode away from the Ransome spread without a backward glance.

By now, at the far end of the trail, the girl was up and running. Sloane's evil face was an impassive mask as he kicked the bay into a canter.

★ ★ ★

Because his main concern was to keep well clear of Reuben Flack, Gade Haggard elected to ride towards the Ransome spread along the blind side of the sloping pine ridge behind the cabin, intending to cut across beyond the trees, circle the ranch buildings and approach them from the rear.

He was still more than a mile from that turn-off point and riding at a gentle lope close under a high, sheer bank when he heard the faint double crack of a sixgun, two shots coming in rapid succession. Face set, he touched his mount with his heels, nudging it into a smooth canter, meanwhile keeping his ears pricked.

The heavier boom of a powerful saddle gun reached him moments later. Instantly, Haggard lashed the horse with the reins, urged it into a fast gallop that rapidly took him away from the rougher ground under the banking and out onto level grassland.

As he did so, the lighter weapon cracked again, a single shot this time. Haggard cursed softly, for the first time using his spurs in an effort to find more speed.

Within minutes the ridge petered out, the pines thinned, and he was able to cut across the rolling grass towards the dusty willows marking the course of the river, then swing back on himself to come up on the ranch.

Almost two miles to the east, far beyond the low buildings, he could see a faint pall of dust. Squinting his eyes against the dazzling orb of the sun that was now well above the horizon, he picked out two mounted figures, moving quickly across his line of vision. Indistinct shapes, seen through the dust and lingering mist.

Two riders — or three? He strained his eyes, couldn't be sure. Then they were gone, hidden by a line of thick scrub.

Flack, with Ames and Diaz. Had to be.

But he knew there was another possibility, and to the terrible fear of what might have happened to Libbie he blanked his mind, allowing himself to think only of what the gunfire he had heard warned him to expect.

Careful to keep the barn between him and the yard, Haggard walked his horse silently across the thick grass, reined in close against the high timber walls and dismounted.

He paused there a moment to listen, head tilted, his back pressed against the barn's cool timbers. Somewhere close by a horse blew through its nostrils. Another whickered uneasily. High above him, the windmill creaked twice, lazily, as a hesitant breeze whispered by, then faded.

Common sense told him he was wasting time with caution. Flack and his men had gone. And with every passing second that brought with it no movement or sound, the other fear that he stubbornly refused to acknowledge became closer to a certainty.

Haggard drew his Army Colt, settled his hat on his head. Then he moved cautiously to the corner of the barn. He was braced, already expecting the worst. Nevertheless, what he saw caused him to clench his teeth against rising sickness, turned his grey eyes hard and cold.

Through the narrow passage between barn and bunkhouse he could see a section of the yard. A booted foot and part of a leg were just visible, lying in the dust, washed by the warm rays of a morning sun their owner would never feel.

Grim-faced, sixgun held high, Haggard made his way cautiously between the buildings. He emerged into bright sunlight. One swift, sweeping glance took in the corral, the dusty yard, the cottonwoods shading the rough timber seat; the bloody corpses.

The old man was spreadeagled in the dust, arms and booted feet outstretched, the sockets of his pale, sightless eyes pooled with congealing blood. Haggard crouched, closed the warm eyelids, with a grimace wiped his fingers on the dead man's shirt.

Still crouched, he glanced across the yard; from thirty feet away looked at the other man, lying sprawled under the cottonwoods. That would be Ransome, he surmised. For the man he had just ministered to was old, a man with the scarred hands and bow legs of a wrangler. He had fought no recent wars. If he had married at all the ceremony would have been in the distant past.

Libbie . . . Libbie . . .

Numb with horror, Haggard straightened, walked across to the warm body that had been Mil Ransome. Again he closed a dead man's eyes, straightened, turned away. But he was hurrying now, narrowed eyes continually searching the yard, the corral, the fringes of grassland, the rutted track.

And all the while his mind was backtracking, recalling a sequence of sounds . . .

Looking for hope.

He had heard two shots in quick succession, fired from a sixgun. Those slugs had smashed into Ransome's chest, knocking him backwards under the dusty trees. The old wrangler had taken one bullet between the eyes and it had blown his brains out the back of his head. That accounted for all three pistol shots.

But between them, Haggard had heard the single, thunderous report of a powerful rifle — and the only explanation he could come up with was that Libbie had seen her husband gunned down, and got off that one shot.

But why no more? And where was she now?

Racking his brains for an answer, finding none, Gade Haggard worked off some of his seething anger by dragging both men into the cool of the open barn, stretching their slack bodies on sweet hay, covering them as best he could with tarps.

And it was not until he emerged into

the sunlight, using his hat to beat the dust and straw from his clothes, that he caught sight of the red ribbon lying midway between the patches of bloodstained dust.

Haggard scrubbed the sweat from his face with his sleeve, picked up the scrap of cloth, rubbed the neatly tied bow with a calloused thumb.

In his imagination he could see the smooth silk slipping, or being dragged, from the blonde hair it had restrained. But in what circumstances? Terror-stricken flight away from the bloodshed? A fierce struggle against a powerful man?

With his finger and thumb, Haggard plucked the single long strand of hair that remained caught in the knot, let it drift away, followed it with his eyes as it floated to the ground, then let his gaze move away to read what he could from the jumbled imprints of boots and hooves in the dust.

Then he turned away in disgust.

No sign was needed to tell this

story. Hell, the whole place stank of a corrupt presence. Reuben Flack had been here, left Ames and Diaz to cover his approach with their saddle guns, the ridden in like a goddamn angel of death to kill the Yankee and seize Libbie. The old wrangler had got in the way and been shot down like a dog.

Behind the barn again, Haggard mounted up, used a single hitch to tie the red ribbon to his saddle horn. With his habitual caution he rode away from the ranch the same way he had come in, circling around to the far side of the ridge before pointing his horse towards the distant town.

The ribbon of silk fluttered before him all the way to Desolation, a personal guidon to remind him of his sister, Libbie, and of how Major Reuben Flack had today ruined her life.

But even as he rode, Gade Haggard sensed that his thinking was all wrong.

8

'Who are you?' Libbie Ransome demanded.

A profusion of fine scratches covered her face, transforming her cheeks and forehead into a scrawled map of bloody lines that she dabbed at continually with her sleeve. Her fair hair was tangled by the fall into the mesquite. The shoulders and back of her shirt were stained and torn from contact with the hard earth.

Yet she rode easily, naturally, allowing the pony to be led by the one-eyed killer on the big bay. Although her eyes were mirrors reflecting the horrors she had witnessed, resilience was repairing the damage, her unquenchable spirit demanding answers. With steely resolve she was banishing the immediate past, courageously confronting the present because, in the hands of this man, her life surely hung by a slender thread.

'Who are you?' she repeated. 'Who . . . who put you up to this . . . ?'

Diamond Jack Sloane allowed the bay to drop back alongside the paint pony. The girl was on his blind side, so that he had to twist his neck to see her. He took in the torn shirt, the tangled hair like ripe, wind-blown corn, the blood-streaked face. He saw the life flowing back into the grey eyes, and grinned his approval.

'Feller called Flack,' he said. 'Paid me in cash money — but what he don't realize is all he's bought hisself is trouble.'

'Reuben Flack,' she whispered, and it was as if the past had returned to slap her in the face.

'Your lovin' step-daddy.'

'He's a murderer!' she blurted; then caught his swift glance and shuddered. This man was a murderer, twice over. Who was he? Where was he taking her?

The fall from the dun had knocked

the breath from her body, the mesquite ripping at her flesh as she crashed through the unyielding, raking branches and hit the packed earth with a jarring thud. Then she had heard the sudden, shocking boom of the big rifle.

Until that moment she had assumed the galloping horse had stepped in a prairie-dog hole, snapped its leg. Realizing that the black-garbed killer had felled it with a single, long-range shot, and was coming after her, she had frantically torn herself from the mesquite's clinging embrace and run for her life.

Where was she going? She had no idea, other than it must be away from the ranch, from the terrible man in black. Her mind was dazed. The image of Mil being blown backwards by the sixgun's blast seared into her brain. She was sick with disbelief. Everything was moving too fast, yet when she tried to run from the danger her legs were so weak she felt as if she were running through deep water.

Then she had become dimly aware of the thunder of approaching hooves swelling in her ears. Fear mounted as the heavy pounding drew unbearably close, became unreal, a nightmare, so that as she ran she clamped her hands to her ears. Her harsh breathing tore at her throat. The pounding hooves were drowned by the thunder of her heart.

Suddenly, the horse was upon her, its hot, snorting breath at her shoulder — and she was falling. Then a strong arm caught her, clamped around her waist and with her last, gasping breath she screamed. But the scream was a whisper, the terror in her mind. She was swung effortlessly off the ground. Her bloody face was pressed against a black shirt that reeked of stale sweat. The hard butt of a holstered sixgun bored painfully into her ribs.

'And you, too, are a murderer,' she said now, boldly, but with a sob catching at her throat. Her memory was becoming clearer, minute by minute, and she said, 'You told my . . . my husband . . . you wouldn't leave without the woman. That means you came to the ranch for me. And you say Reuben Flack put you up to it, is paying you in gold?'

He laughed softly, his single eye ranging ahead.

The horses were moving at a comfortable walk, had been since he had shaken her brutally to bring her to her senses, then transferred her from his own horse to the paint pony.

He had run her down at the edge of the mesquite thickets. From there they had ridden steadily west over land that sloped gently towards the river. Now he guided the horses down through trailing willows and into the gravel shallows under the low, sandy banks. The sun was at their backs, glistening on the clear water as they followed the river's course.

'Did you hear what I said?'

'Sure,' he said, standing in the stirrups to gaze into the distance. 'But it's a complicated issue.'

'If he paid you to kidnap me, and you have — where's the complication?'

'He paid me — but not for that.'

Leather creaked as he settled back in the saddle. He reined in, and the two horses dipped their heads and began to drink.

'My name's Jack Sloane,' he said, studying her face. 'That mean anything to you?'

'Should it?'

He shrugged. 'Years ago, Flack was followed when he rode into the Staked Plains. The name of the man chasin' him was clear enough in Flack's mind when he met up with your ma. He might have told her what wickedness he'd done to make a man follow him through that white hell, maybe yelled out in his dreams.'

'You?' she asked, saw the slow, negative shake of his head and as memory again came flooding back she gasped, said, 'Before you shot him you told Mil . . . you told my husband you wanted two men dead. One of them was Flack! Is that because of what happened, all those years ago?'

He nodded, his eyes on a distant column of smoke rising into the clear skies.

'And my brother?' She bit her lip, trembling, said, 'Perhaps I can understand your need to kill Reuben Flack, but why would anyone want to shoot Gade?' She frowned, her mind racing. 'It's Flack, isn't it? He hanged my brothers. Now he wants Gade dead. He paid you to do it, without realizing that you hold something against him, hate him.'

He twisted to look at her, said, 'That's a part of it — but I'm not going to hurt you, girl.'

'You've already done that by murdering my husband. But remember this: that big gun you carry kills at a distance, but it's also lethal at short range.'

'What the hell's that supposed to mean?'

'It means that if I get hold of it — I'll kill you.'

She looked into the glittering black eye, and the seething hatred caused her to flinch. She knew that quite soon she must back up her words with action, for this man was lying. Something sinister in his past was a threat to her family. She had already witnessed too much for him to allow her to live.

Her real father had died when she was ten years old. Three years later the dust-caked figure of the man called Reuben Flack had appeared out of the shimmering heat haze. He had used his charms to win the heart of Grace Haggard, her lonely mother, but at thirteen Libbie Haggard had been woman enough to recognize the burning desire in his eyes when he looked at her.

Young Will Haggard had ridden out within days, unwilling to play second fiddle to the stranger who had taken the place of his pa. Word of his wanderings had drifted back to them. In time, the boy had carved a reputation for himself, the Will had been dropped in favour of Renegade, and he had grown into a hard and dangerous man.

But his going had been a wasted gesture. Reuben Flack's professed love for Grace Haggard had barely outlasted the working honeymoon. Within six months he had gone, riding away into a storm-tossed night and, cruelly, taking with him the family's life savings.

Gradually, all news of Gade Haggard had dried up. When war broke out, his ma guessed he would enlist, and she persuaded the man called Shako Gunn, then ranch foreman, to go find him. He succeeded. But he also found Reuben Flack, and witnessed a double hanging.

Now, the man from the Staked Plains had come back into her life. Was he yet again the harbinger of death?

'All right,' Libbie said. 'You're not going to hurt me. But you are going to kill Flack and I can only get in the way — so why don't you let me go?'

Without answering, Sloane nudged

the bay with his heels. It moved off, splashing through the shallow water, closely followed by Libbie's paint. Fifty yards further on a section of the bank had crumbled. Sloane sent the bay scrambling up the loose earth and onto a steep slope leading to a stand of old cottonwoods and pecans.

He led the way through brush and deadfalls until they had a clearer view of the surrounding countryside. Again he reined in, pointed ahead a mile or so to where the river formed a wide loop.

'See that smoke?'

Libbie nodded.

'Reuben Flack's camp.' He grinned wickedly. 'Now, what I aim to do is go down there, sort of attract his attention.'

'You're going to use that buffalo gun to kill him.'

'No, ma'am. I'm going to send one of them heavy slugs whistlin' so close to his ear he'll know exactly what it is — and I'll be close enough for him to see who's doin' the shootin'.'

And suddenly, Libbie knew exactly why Jack Sloane needed her. 'Right,' he said softly, watching her face. 'I've got Flack's gold, and that's bad enough. But what he wants more than that, what he's always wanted . . . is you!'

★ ★ ★

The sun was high and hot in a clear blue sky when Gade Haggard dismounted, tied his horse outside the ramshackle café on the edge of Desolation and strode inside. Shako Gunn was in the corner, blanket draped over his chair, chewing on a greasy slab of fried beef as tough as shoe leather and washing it down with black, bitter coffee.

Haggard dragged a chair out across the table from Gunn, straddled it and ordered his own drink. When the greasy-aproned café owner brought him the steaming mug he took a deep draught, choked, swore softly.

'It ain't killed you,' he commented, 'so I guess it only tastes like snake venom.'

Gunn wiped gravy from his empty plate with a hunk of bread, pushed the plate away and settled back.

'Maybe it's one of them slow actin' poisons,' he said, eyes hooded. 'Bides its time, then sneaks up on you when your guard's down.' He dug in his shirt pocket, came out with the makings, tossed the sack on the table. 'Sorta like Reuben Flack,' he said, and watched impassively as Haggard began to fashion a cigarette.

Haggard nodded, his eyes distant. 'The bastard was in and out before the mornin' sun was clear of the trees,' he said. He struck a match, blew a stream of smoke at the flies circling the hanging lamp. 'Killed his Yankee, and a harmless old wrangler,' he went on, looking at Gunn. 'Took Libbie with him when he left.'

'Flack?' Gunn raised his eyebrows, sighed, folded the sack of tobacco and tucked it back in his shirt. 'Nah. The major rode out two, three hours ago. Headed west t'ward the loop in the river. Him and the Mex, and that feller you tangled with.'

'Ames,' Haggard said. He studied the glowing end of his cigarette, said thoughtfully, 'All right. So Flack's in the clear. But someone was out at the Ransome spread, shot him twice, his wrangler once, plumb between the eyes.' He listened to the rattle of dishes in the kitchen, a woman singing; remembered the dusty yard, the still, bloody bodies under the cloudless skies . . . A dark figure, riding out by moonlight . . .

'But he was ridin' in the wrong direction,' he said softly, then shrugged at Gunn's questioning glance. 'I heard pistol shots when I was approachin' the Ransome place. That adds up; both men were killed by someone pretty handy with a sixgun. But in amongst those shots there was the single, heavy blast of a long rifle. Big, powerful gun.'

'Well, we both know a feller who's kinda handy with a Hawken,' Gunn said, grinning. 'Only Sam Pickens told me he's given up shootin' Yankees — and anyway, he don't get up much before noon.'

Almost before the words were out, the door slammed open and Sam Pickens burst in ahead of a flurry of dust, beard as wild as a bird's nest caught in a storm, blue eyes glinting.

' 'Ceptin today,' he said in answer to Gunn's overheard comment. ' 'Cos today, old friends, I reckon I smell trouble in the air, hear ugly rumours bein' circulated.'

'Thought you was deaf?' Gunn said, winking at Haggard.

'Hear what I want to hear,' Pickens said flatly. He squinted past them, yelled, 'Ham and eggs, pronto, Dougie!' towards the smoke-hazed kitchen, then sat down and reached across to shake Haggard's hand and gaze at him quizzically. 'You through lickin' your wounds?'

119

'If you're referrin' to what happened in the war, sure, I'm over it.' He released the old soldier's hand, said, 'Thanks for your help, Sam. Couldn't say much yesterday, but your slug whistlin' through the window sure got me out of a tight spot.'

'Had me a bead on the blond feller. That hot lead would've solved all your problems if I hadn't sneezed,' Pickens complained. 'Shut my eyes, jerked the trigger, damn near fell backwards down the ladder.'

'And on that note,' Gunn said drily, 'we're back on the subject of long rifles.'

Sam's breakfast arrived. Gunn leaned back, again dragged out the makings, placed them alongside Sam's plate.

'This rider I saw, late last night,' Gade Haggard said slowly. 'Tall man, dressed all in black. Light was bad, but seems to me he was carryin' a Sharps Buffalo.'

'But headin' in the wrong direction?'

Haggard caught the change in tone,

looked sharply at Gunn.

'Looked to me like he was leavin' for good — but I reckon you know different?'

Gunn snorted disdainfully. 'Flack told me he hired a man could kill us both without raisin' a sweat. Seems he favours black . . . and totes a big gun.' Frowning, he poked his empty mug with his finger, said, 'So far, that makes sense, Gade. But Flack likes to do his own Yankee killin'. This hired gun doin' it don't ring true.'

'And why take Libbie?'

Gunn nodded. 'I can think of reasons. For starters, Flack knows you'll go gunnin' for anyone lays hands on your sister — and he's always been keen to do that. But if he is usin' her as bait, he's complicating what started out as a simple issue. Hell, Flack could've plugged you hisself, yesterday, but held his fire. And 'stead of ridin' to the Ransome spread on a fool's errand, this gunslinger could've snuck up and killed you in your bed.'

'Sure.' Haggard pursed his lips, his grey eyes perplexed. 'I can't figure it. If a man uses bait to catch a wild crittur, he plants it where it'll be found. But right now we don't even know where Libbie's bein' held — don't even know for sure she *has* been taken. Hell, if she somehow managed to get to a fast horse she could be halfway to Castle Gap by now!'

'All ifs and maybes,' Sam Pickens mumbled around a mouthful of salty bacon, 'Here's another. Maybe Flack's roped hisself a maverick.'

Gunn cocked an eyebrow. 'Meanin'?'

'Feller Flack's hired to kill you an' Gade is Diamond Jack Sloane,' Pickens said. He pushed his plate away, belched, said, 'Flack paid him up front, in gold. Now, the only person that makes sense to is the man bein' paid to do the killin'. With his pockets weighed down with double eagles, any reasonable man'd take the easy course.'

'He'd forget the job, and ride on,'

Shako Gunn said softly.

'Instead,' Haggard said, 'he's killed two men who weren't part of any deal and — maybe — kidnapped my sister.'

He watched Pickens pour a line of strong dark tobacco along a paper, roll the cigarette; looked into the sharp blue eyes, said, 'Why, Sam?'

Sam Pickens stuck the cigarette in the corner of his mouth, tossed the sack of tobacco to Shako Gunn, slapped his palms on the table.

'Other than Diamond Jack Sloane,' he said, 'the only man might know the answer to that one is camped down where the river bends.'

9

They'd left Ames's ragged, long-haired brother in charge of the six-horse remuda. A lanky, bone-thin youth, he had been a drummer with the Confederate cavalry during the war. Cruelly exposed to years of violent action, he had witnessed enough savage blood-letting to bleach all feeling from his eyes, leaving them with a flat blankness devoid of all hope.

At the first, faint rattle of approaching riders, he had slipped silently away into the thin stand of trees close to the water.

When Flack and his gunslingers rode in along the riverbank, the camp in the small clearing appeared deserted. A thin column of smoke from the campfire rose into the clear air. The only sounds were the crackle of burning mesquite, the rush of fast-flowing waters, the sudden, welcoming whicker from one of the tethered horses.

Flack dismounted, hung the reins over the pommel, let his horse wander down to the river. He strutted over to the fire, with his gloved hand took hold of the blackened pot hanging in the licking flames, tipped scalding coffee into a tin mug he found lying in the grass.

Behind him, Ames yelled, 'Frank!', and as Diaz wandered across to stand spread-legged by the fire the youngster emerged sheepishly from the trees, thrusting a big sixgun into the holster tied down to his skinny thigh.

'I was bein' careful, like you told me — '

'See anything?' Flack demanded, cutting him short.

'Maybe. I cain't be sure.'

'Hell, kid, either you saw something, or you didn't.'

'Go easy, Major,' Ames said.

'Easy!' Flack swung on Ames, his face set. 'With Haggard and Gunn on the loose, I take no chances.'

'Gunn's in town, watching his back,' Diaz said, squatting to poke at the flames with a stick. 'Him and the trigger-happy ostler, both.'

'Yeah, an' that fancy gunslinger's gonna take care of Haggard,' Ames mocked, winking at the Mexican. 'If he ain't already lit out with all that gold.'

Flack shook his head. 'No. Jack Sloane wants Haggard for himself.'

'So what will he do, Major?' Diaz asked. 'Will he bring you Haggard's ears as proof of his skill?' He had moved away from the fire and was sitting against the bole of a tree, his big sombrero tipped forward over his eyes.

'Yeah,' the boy, Frank, said, his face suddenly eager. 'Maybe that was him, waitin' out there, Major. Only, I couldn't figure it 'cos there was two of them an' — '

All three men heard the sudden, sickening thwack of a bullet hitting solid flesh, watched in stunned disbelief

126

as the boy, knocked off his feet by the tremendous blow, was flung backwards. He fell on his back in the dust. One hand flopped into the fire and at once there was the smell of singed cloth and burning flesh.

More than a second later, the distant boom of a heavy rifle carried to them through the hot, still air.

'Jesus!'

Diaz rolled clumsily away from the tree, came to his feet fumbling for his sixgun. Crouching low, Ames ran to his brother, caught hold of his free arm and dragged him clear of the flames. Releasing the slack form he continued on across the clearing to his horse, slid the Spencer out of its boot, moved quickly to the edge of the trees.

Bright sunlight slanted through the branches, hampering vision. Heat devils danced over rocks in the middle distance. Far away, light flashed, and was gone.

Ames jacked a shell into the rifle's breech, said tersely to Diaz, 'You spotted the bushwhackin' bastard?'

'Downstream, in from the river, alongside the trees atop that low rise.'

'Yeah,' Ames gritted. 'I see him.'

'And that's about all you can do,' Diaz said bitterly.

'Sharps Buffalo?'

'Sure. Well out of range.'

Then, in the tense stillness, a thin voice drifted to them, carrying across the open country like the hunting cry of a wild animal.

'Flack! Reuben Flack!'

'I hear you, Jack Sloane!' Flack roared. He flung the tin mug across the clearing, moved to the edge of the trees and stepped out into the open, lifted a hand to squint into the sun.

'You out of your mind, Major?' Ames snarled, and snapped two, three rapid, futile shots towards the rise, then two more. Dust spurted in the sparse dry grass, a long way short. Then the branches overhead twitched as a slug hummed through the air and continued on; high, mocking, its passing punctuated by the bellow of the heavy Sharps.

'He's done with killing for now,' Flack stated, legs braced, hands on hips. 'Grabbed our attention with that first shot — but what the hell's his game?'

'The kid died tellin' the truth,' Diaz said, and flashed him a glance. 'There's two of 'em out there.'

'An' one's a woman,' Ames said.

'The devil you say,' Flack breathed. His horse, watered now, had ambled up the slope from the river. Flack crossed swiftly to it, unbuckled a saddlebag and reached in for his field-glasses, strode back through the trees and clapped the glasses to his eyes; swore softly, bitterly.

'Got that purty Ransome woman, right?' Ames taunted, watching him.

'Shut your goddamned mouth!'

'Nights're cold,' Diaz said pleasantly. 'A man needs something soft, keep him warm, happy . . . '

Flack swung away, face set, eyes

129

narrowed, speculative. He stared unseeing at Diaz, Ames, turned to gaze towards the distant gunman, said, 'There's more to it than that. I paid him to kill Haggard. Instead he rode to the Ransome spread, must've taken the girl by force. Why do that? And why ride here, kill a man for no reason?'

Diaz twirled his Remington, spun it expertly into its holster, hunkered down patiently. 'You already part worked that out, Major. My guess is you know the rest. Sloane pocketed your gold, took your woman. Now he's got your attention — but you know damn well killin' Ames's brother's told you more'n that.'

'I know,' Flack said. 'But I don't know why.'

'The man's tellin' you you're next,' Ames said, thumbing shells into the Spencer's butt magazine. 'Ain't anything more you need to know.'

'That's the way I had her figured,' Diaz agreed happily. 'An' right now the black clad sonofabitch's out there takin' a bead on the major's broad chest, gettin' ready to squeeze the trigger.'

Reuben Flack shook his head, spat contemptuously.

'No. Not yet. He wants me to sweat. In some way the girl's involved in this, and if she is then that ties in Gade Haggard. But where does Jack Sloane fit in? What's the link between him and the girl — and why is he gunning for me — ?'

Abruptly his words were chopped short and he jerked in shock and fell awkwardly back into the trees as a second slug smacked into flesh and one of the remuda horses went down, kicking. The report followed swiftly, the deep boom almost covering the sound of another slug hitting home. A second tethered horse squealed in terror, and crashed into the scrub.

Then Ames was across the clearing. He reached the picket rope, slipped it free, then dashed his hat from his · head and slapped it madly against his pants, yipping and yelling to send the remaining horses galloping away down the riverbank. They hammered across the loose gravel, hit the shallow water hard. Flying spray glittered in the bright sun.

'Ain't never seen a man with a Sharps Buffalo reload that fast,' Diaz marvelled.

As the rattle of hooves faded, the voice of Diamond Jack Sloane reached them, much closer now. His tone was hard, filled with menace.

'You gettin' jumpy, Flack?'

'What the hell do you want?'

A laugh rang out; cold, brittle.

'Two lives, Major.'

'One must be Haggard. And I already paid you good money to finish him.' Flack glanced around at Ames and Diaz, snapped, 'If he's close enough, use your rifles.' Then called loudly, 'I'm a reasonable man, Sloane. What you do after downing Haggard is your affair.'

Nodding to the two gunslingers, he drew his ivory-handled .45. Then, bent over, he threaded his way through the trees until they thinned and the sun was hot on his face; heard the crack of a breaking branch as Diaz worked his way around to the left, the snap of oiled metal as Ames worked the lever and jacked a shell into the Spencer's breech.

Then Flack looked up, and drew a sharp, shocked breath.

Diamond Jack Sloane was no more than fifty yards away, a gaunt black figure sitting silent and still atop a rangy bay. Libbie Ransome was alongside him, stiffly upright on a paint pony, looking lost and forlorn beside the gunman on the big horse.

In the sun's hot glare her face was white and set. Her head was tilted a little to one side as she strained away from the muzzle of the big Sharps. Sloane held the rifle relaxed and easy across his thighs. The muzzle was rammed against the ridge of bone behind Libbie Ransome's left ear.

A crimson bandanna was bound tightly across her mouth.

'Put up your gun, Major, tell those fools to do the same,' Sloane ordered. 'If I die, she dies, and you don't want that.'

Anger flared in Reuben Flack. He took a deep breath, holstered his pistol, gestured to Ames and Diaz, said, 'Do as he says.'

'All right,' Sloane called. 'Now listen hard. I rode here so you could see the situation. The whys and wherefores and the reasoning behind what I'm doing are for you to work out. While you're busy scratchin' your head, I'll be doin' some serious ridin'.' He paused, jerked a thumb over his shoulder, grinned wolfishly. 'And, I tell you, Flack, that's something I'm lookin' forward to, because I'll have this sweet young woman with me to make those long nights under the stars a pleasurable experience.'

'You touch her,' Reuben Flack yelled hoarsely, 'and I'll find you, and kill you.'

'Hoped you'd say that,' Sloane

said, nodding his approval. 'Means your thinking's takin' the right track, although so far the reason for it heading that way is the wrong one.'

'You're talkin' in riddles, Sloane, actin' like a man totin' a broad yellow streak. I didn't have you figured for a man'd hide behind a woman. Let her go, get your grudge out in the open then face me like a man!'

'There ain't no need for us to listen, no reason to talk a load of bullshit,' Ames said from the edge of the trees. 'We could take him, easy. One shot, like he took my kid brother.'

'Let him talk!'

'First Gunn, now Jack Sloane,' Diaz yelled derisively. 'You're lettin' too many men talk, then walk away from you, Major.'

Diamond Jack Sloane laughed. 'You see, the girl means nothing to them, Flack, just like she means nothing to me 'cept as something to be used. But they're right, we're wasting time.'

Unexpectedly, he put heels to his

horse, wheeled both ill-matched mounts to face the opposite direction in a precise cavalry manoeuvre that under different circumstances would have earned Flack's approval. Then, with a touch of the spurs he set the horses to a fast walk and, leather creaking, metalwork flashing in the sun, they began to move steadily away from the trees and the river.

And all the while the deadly Sharps Buffalo was held rock steady against the girl's head.

Then, suddenly, Diamond Jack Sloane's anger spilled over. He swung in the saddle, roared over his shoulder, 'So's you'll have something to chew on, the way I'm pointed now is the way I'll stay pointed. Now all you do is figure where that leads, and then you start lookin' back in your mind and you'll know when this started, where it's gotta finish — and why the second of those lives I mentioned is yours.'

And then he was gone, a haze of dust drifting towards the river, and Ames was alongside Reuben Flack, down on one knee, his cheek tight against the Spencer's stock as he lined the sights on the taller of the two rapidly receding riders.

Flack's jaw bunched. As Diaz brushed through the long grass towards him, Flack drew his .45 and struck Ames a vicious, swinging blow across the back of the head. The gunman collapsed without a sound. His nerveless finger jerked the trigger. The rifle discharged harmlessly into the high blue skies.

'The Staked Plains,' Reuben Flack mused aloud, absently kicking the downed gunslinger. 'That's where he's takin' her, and that's the route I took to Comanche Springs and the Haggards. But how in hell're the Staked Plains a link between me and Diamond Jack Sloane?'

* * *

From their vantage point on a high, wide escarpment a mile or so west of

Desolation, Haggard and his companions saw the two mounted figures they had watched ride from the tree-covered rise to the open grassland bordering the tributary of the Concho as black dots, the Sharps Buffalo as nothing more than a brilliant shaft of reflected light.

But the big gun's detonations had been unmistakable. Gade Haggard's skin had turned cold as the thunder of the shots was carried on the hot air and he recalled those earlier reports he had heard in the cool clear light after dawn; the blood-caked bodies he had left to the hordes of flies in the dust alongside Mil Ransome's spread.

Oh, there was little doubt that this man using a Sharps .45-.120 to pin down Flack and his men in their camp by the placid river was the man who had fired those shots, and so a cold-blooded killer.

And it was now certain that he had Libbie.

'She worshipped me, that girl,'

Haggard said softly. 'Those last months, spring comin' in with warming winds and the purest, clearest rain you ever saw, she had pigtails and freckles and skinny legs and I was a clumsy kid blind to everything 'less it had four legs and wore a Mexican saddle. But she followed me everywhere. If she cut her knee on a rock, I'd wash away the blood. If she cried, I'd dry her tears.

'Then one day Reuben Flack came a-ridin' out of the Staked Plains, face cracked, yeller hair stringy and that fancy gun on his hip and I was so big and so strong — such a big, brave man — I turned tail, walked out on my sister even though I'd seen the look in that man's eyes, even then knowing it for pure lust . . . '

'Flack ain't got her,' Shako Gunn said flatly. 'Diamond Jack Sloane's took her, and he must have a mighty good reason.'

Sam Pickens was a crumpled figure on an unkempt black gelding, battered cavalry hat pinned up at the front with a sharp thorn, one booted foot hooked over the saddle horn. He was rolling a quirly, his sharp blue eyes slitted as he gazed into the distance.

'Seems to me you're two parts of the way there in your thinking, Gade,' the old ostler said. He struck a match, sucked on the cigarette, squinted thoughtfully at the blue smoke. 'Both you and Flack're connected to that gal in one way or another. That leaves Diamond Jack. 'Stead of killin' you like he was told to do, he rode out, took that gal. He must know it won't take you long to find out. In the meantime he's rode down there with her so Flack can see what a clever *hombre* he is.'

'And that done — he's hightailed,' Shako Gunn said, and jerked his head to where the two dots were now steadily dragging a thin plume of dust towards the western horizon.

'Where's he from?'

Pickens flicked Haggard a glance, shrugged. 'Southern Texas, mostly. Laredo, Mex border country.'

'So why ride west?'

Shako Gunn chuckled. 'Questions, questions.' He flipped his blanket away from his hip, dragged a canteen from his saddle-bag, took a swallow, shook his head. 'The girl's a lure, Gade; she's bait, you know that. Right now it don't matter a damn which way Sloane's goin'. What he's doin' is leadin' you and the major a dance. Christ knows why, but seems to me there's only one way you're going to find out.'

'Flack's breaking camp,' Sam Pickens said sharply.

For long moments there was silence from the watching men broken now and then by the gentle blowing of the horses, the lazy scuffle of a hoof, the rattle as Gunn replaced his canteen.

'Got a grave to dig first. That'll take time,' Gade Haggard said tightly. 'We'll sit tight, watch them move out. After that . . . well, I made promises to that girl, and so far I ain't made a great shape at keepin' 'em.'

'An' forgettin' all about promises, kept, broken or just plain forgotten, it's your sister he's got so what the hell else can we do but go after the varmint?' Sam Pickens said.

'We?'

Off to one side, Shako Gunn chuckled richly. 'Now I come to think of it, in the early days of the war, every time I found myself diggin' latrines or up at dawn helpin' with chow — it was this little runt'd volunteered me for the job.'

'You outrank us both now, Sergeant,' Haggard said gruffly. He wanted to thank both men, but unable to find the words he was content to indulge in the familiar banter that had held them together, sustained them, through the those bloody years of strife.

'That bein' the case,' Gunn said, stowing his canteen with a flamboyant swirl of his blanket, 'I'll countermand your last order. We're one up on Flack:

we've seen him, he ain't seen us. So leave him to bury his dead. By the time he's in the saddle we'll've cut around that rise, outflanked him, and be five miles down the trail.'

Part Three

The Pursuit

10

Three miles west of Flack's camp, Diamond Jack Sloane turned the galloping horses across a wide loop in the trail and they ploughed into an expanse of loose dirt. The fine dust kicked up by the big dun at once threatened to blind the closely following paint. Libbie twisted her head to one side as her eyes began to stream. She coughed against the tight gag, then began to retch.

As the horses began labouring, Diamond Jack used the trail rope to pull the blowing paint tight up against his stirrup, then leaned out of the saddle and ripped away the red bandanna that was binding Libbie's mouth. When she grabbed it from him with both hands and used the damp cloth to clean her eyes and wipe her hot, sticky face, he grinned, dragged a hand across his own dry mouth and reached for his canteen.

He slaked his thirst, then passed the canteen to her and she scrubbed the neck before putting it to her mouth and gulping thirstily at the warm water. All the while, Sloane shifted impatiently in his saddle and cast darting glances back down the trail with his one glittering eye, a half-smile fixed on his gaunt face.

'There was no need for this,' Libbie gasped, droplets of water glistening on her quivering lips. 'I had nothing to say to that man, had no thought of warning him.' She flung the bandanna forcefully at him, watched him catch it as it flapped against his face, saw the amusement in his eye and knew that nothing she could say or do would touch this man.

'So Reuben Flack knows now,' she continued shakily. 'That's part of what you wanted and maybe he'll come after me, maybe not. But what about my brother? You came to my house soon after sunup . . . ' She paused, biting her lip at bitter memories of gunfire and spilt blood and the horrors of death, went on shakily, 'You came soon after sun-up, then avoided Desolation by cutting across country to the bend in the river. Gade cannot know that.'

'He'll know,' Sloane said without concern.

With a last searching look down the trail, he took the canteen from her, packed it away and urged the horses into a fast canter. This time he let her ride alongside, out of his dust.

The river began to swing towards the south, and to maintain their westerly direction they moved away from its rolling banks and the horses again quit the trail. Heads held high they eagerly cut across hockdeep, rolling grassland.

After a while, Libbie said, 'You're using me as bait so you can kill my brother.' She laughed shortly. 'The day he left home he came to me, warned me then of Reuben Flack. He promised me that one day he would come back and we'd be together. This is the first time in all those years that we've been close, yet I pray to God he sees through your ruse and stays away.'

Sloane sat back in the swaying saddle, held his elbows high as he expertly fashioned a cigarette. 'I hear he's carryin' a heap of guilt over what Flack did to his brothers in the war. That's likely to push him hard in this direction.'

'God help him,' she said softly, with deep compassion. 'None of his family or friends blame him for that, each and every one of us has lived with the bitter truth; the knowledge that Flack came to our home and like fools, we trusted him.'

'Oh, the bitter truth is that one way or another both Reuben Flack and Gade Haggard're as guilty as hell,' Jack Sloane said, his voice tight with suppressed fury.

There was silence then, and for

most of the next three hours, Sloane punishing horses and riders as he forced a furious pace to put miles between them and Reuben Flack and — he anticipated — the vengeful Gade Haggard. They rode with their drawn faces staring into the glare of the afternoon sun, the mismatched horses stretching out valiantly as Jack Sloane ruthlessly applied spurs to the dun and towed the tiring paint along at the end of the short lead rope. And as the miles fell away beneath the pounding hooves it was noticeable that the temperature rose as the cooling waters of the river were left behind, the low hills gradually receded and the landscape became uniformly flat, the heat a dancing, shimmering curtain blurring the horizon.

'Where are we going?' Libbie gasped suddenly.

Sloane grunted. 'You're a Haggard; you tell me.'

'Yes,' she said, wearily twitching back her damp hair as her eyes cast

151

about at the increasing monotony of the land then turned again towards the distant, uneven smudge on the western horizon that even the heat haze could not hide. 'We're heading for the Llano Estacado.'

'Staked Plains.' He nodded. And a few minutes later, as if coming to a sudden decision, he straightened in the saddle and began to ease their pace, eventually drawing both flagging, lathered mounts to an unsteady halt alongside a wide, grassy depression, an oval hollow in the prairie where clear water had collected in a shallow pool, the eastern lip of which was ridged with exposed bedrock.

'You intend to kill Reuben Flack,' she said, watching him slide from the saddle, slap dust from his black outfit, stretch the kinks out of his joints. 'Why? A long time ago, Flack reached Comanche Springs after an arduous crossing of the plains. We knew there had been some kind of trouble; he mentioned it without going into details, said it was of no consequence — but you weren't involved, couldn't have been.'

Her face wore a puzzled frown as she stepped down heavily out of the saddle.

Without answering he led the horses off the wide, flat trail and down the gentle slope, ground tethered them in the lush grass, then stripped his rig and dumped it close to a couple of stunted live oaks. When he'd unsaddled the paint, he set about gathering wood and building a fire.

'Vittles in the saddle-bags,' he said curtly. 'Flour, sow-belly, coffee.'

She knew it was useless talking, questioning. Suddenly conscious of a gnawing hunger, she swilled cold water over her face at the pool then set to and rustled up a meal and they ate voraciously and in silence, hunkered down some distance apart on either side of the crackling fire, sharing that meal yet forever separated by the bleak memory of a mindless killing that had made her a widow.

Though she could not condone it, she supposed that he had strong reasons for wanting Reuben Flack and Gade dead, and for him that would justify the killing. But she had watched him gun down her husband because he wanted her for bait, had seen that the deed itself amused him, and that was incomprehensible, unforgivable, the act of a cold-blooded killer for whom all life was cheap.

As she sipped her coffee she caught Jack Sloane watching her. His face was gaunt, his single black eye glittering, the silken ribbons of his patch dangling across his strong, lean neck. He was sitting with his hands resting on his spread knees, wrists limp, and she saw in the deep grass between his booted legs the long, blued barrel of the Sharps Buffalo, and she shuddered.

As if reading her innermost thoughts, as if no time had passed since she questioned him, he said in a harsh monotone, 'Reuben Flack raped my sister. She died in childbirth. My grief-stricken father died pursuing Flack across the Staked Plains.'

She watched the limp wrists stiffen, the hands clench into fists; felt her mind sink into the stillness of pure horror.

'In San Miguel,' Sloane went on, 'a six-year-old kid walked into the middle of a gunfight and took a slug in the chest. He was my son. He died in the blood-soaked dust of that street. The man who killed him was Gade Haggard.'

'An accident,' Libbie whispered, appalled. 'It must have been, surely you can see that . . . '

'Accident — but no less dead,' Sloane said flatly.

'What . . . what are you going to do?'

Diamond Jack Sloane picked up the heavy rifle, ran his palms along the smooth barrel, balanced it across his knees.

'As they come riding in I'm going

to pick off their companions,' he said. 'One by one. That'll make the men left alive a mite wary. But still they'll come after me, and always I'll be falling back until there's only one place to go. The final showdown'll be in the place of my choosing.' He jerked his head. 'Out there, where the bones of my father lie bleaching in the white dust and baking heat of the Staked Plains.'

'You'll be outnumbered. They'll come at you from all sides!'

'They won't even get close. And as men begin to die, Reuben Flack and Gade Haggard will have time and reason to recall their sins.'

'Have . . . have you no pity?'

'Back in San Miguel,' he said bluntly, 'there's a fine, white-haired lady dressed all in black bin growing' old mournin' her husband and daughter.'

'Do you dress for mourning? Or is that the garb of a harbinger of death?' Her laugh was brittle. 'Never mind. Nothing you say justifies any of this. And what do you suppose I'll be doing while you're . . . while you're shooting down these men?'

'Flack being an army major, I reckon he'll make his move at dawn. That suits me. At that hour men's bodies're awake but their minds're still tucked in their blankets. When they come ridin' in out of the eastern sun I'll spot them a mile away — but you, gal, will be tied to one of those oaks, with that red bandanna tight across your pretty lips.'

As he spoke his eye had turned towards the low rimrock, the limitless expanse of grassland, as if already seeing the black specks of phantom horsemen. Then, in a gesture that at other times would have been insignificant but now was filled with grim intent, he reached across to his saddle-bags, took out a small oil bottle and soft cloths, and began to work on the deadly firing mechanism of the big Sharps Buffalo.

★ ★ ★

157

Diamond Jack Sloane worked on the rifle as the red sun went down beyond the high ragged horizon that was the edge of the elevated tableland known as the Staked Plains, and she watched him gather together the English Curtis and Harvey powder, the paper-patched bullets he told her were of the right mix of lead and tin to penetrate flesh, then mushroom; watched him fix the Vollmer telescopic sight to the blued barrel and knew that everything he had told her was the truth.

And she knew, too, that she could not allow him to do this, not to her brother, not to the unknown men who rode with him; not, even, to the man known as Reuben Flack, who had inflicted infinite pain and grief on her family but could not, must not, be cut down like a mad dog.

As the dying sun turned the skies over the prairie to gold, Libbie Ransome hugged her knees and thought of her dead husband and, for a little while, gave way to her grief. But as she wept scalding tears there in the shadows of the live oaks, in another, fiercely determined part of her mind the young woman who was now a widow plotted and schemed to prevent murder.

11

'Camp-fire ahead.'

Ames was fifty yards in the lead on a long, gentle downslope, riding hard, sitting canted forward in the saddle with reins held high and the Spencer thrust out wide like a lance in his right hand.

As he shouted the warning he hauled on the reins and dragged his bronc to a slithering stop, peered away at an angle to his left. So keen was he to come up with the black-clad killer who had murdered his brother that he seemed to be sniffing the night air.

Then, as his narrowed eyes confirmed that the pinprick of light was a small fire flickering under squat trees silhouetted against the red disc of the sinking sun, the rifle was punched aloft in triumph and he spun his horse and galloped back to Flack and Diaz.

'About where I figured they'd be,' Reuben Flack said.

He stood in the stirrups, glanced about him, surveying a prairie that appeared flat in daylight but was transformed by the setting sun into an undulating landscape casting a thousand dark, creeping shadows.

The camp-fire was no more than three or four hundred yards away, but a straggling line of parched trees intruded on their line of sight and a low hillock hid part of the campsite.

'Over yonder,' Diaz said suddenly, pointing. 'We see better from there.'

Flack swung about, spotted the shallow, rocky arroyo with a convenient ridge of higher ground on its far side, grunted his satisfaction, then put spurs to his horse and rode across the intervening hundred yards and down into the shelter of the draw.

As the others caught up, drew rein, swung out of the saddle and ground-tethered the horses, Flack led the way on foot up to the high ground, dislodged rocks clattering into the draw so that the horses whinnied, and pawed nervously.

'They are too far away to hear,' Diaz said, white teeth flashing under his dark moustache. 'And if they hear, what can they do?'

'Three, four hundred yards, and all that's left for Jack Sloane is a heap of dyin',' Ames said, and he hunkered down, began a rapid check of the Spencer.

'What can you see, Diaz?' Flack's long hair was tinged with gold as he stood on the highest vantage point, peering west into the sun. But his eyes were old and tired, and he swore in frustration, turned impatiently to the Mexican.

'Two horses,' Diaz said.

'That's them!' Ames exulted, and he ran, stumbling in his haste, to a big, flat-topped boulder.

'Easy, now, easy,' Flack said softly, but his cruel eyes were flashing in triumph as he saw Diaz nod slowly and with certainty.

'The light gives them away,' the Mexican said, the big sombrero tilted so that the wide brim shaded his eyes. 'Two figures only. I saw them moving — look, now, you can see them, Ames. One of them is wearing a skirt. But, see, she has now moved away — sat down, I think — and there is just the tall one, by the horses.'

'I see him,' Ames hissed.

He was down on one knee at the corner of the boulder. In that position — half straddling the stone — he was able to use the solid rock as a support for both his elbows. Now he lowered his cheek to the Spencer, clamped the butt into his shoulder, peered along the sights.

Diaz was right, Ames realized, and his skin prickled with excitement. The evening light had betrayed Jack Sloane. Everything in the campsite was pin sharp: the horses, the delicate tracery of the trees' branches, the thin plume of smoke — the tall figure tending to the big horse, silhouetted against the crimson skies.

Ames bared his teeth, flashed a ferocious leer at the Mexican; settled himself, took a slow, shallow breath, held it — and carefully squeezed the trigger.

'Gotcha, you sonofabith!' Diaz yelled.

The blast of the big Spencer split the night like a crack of thunder. The flash was a brilliant flare of lightning. But as their ears sang and a red blotch danced before their eyes as they peered into the dusk, there was no mistaking the effect of the shot.

Alongside the big horse the tall figure jerked, stiffened, then crumpled to the ground.

'All right,' Reuben Flack said. 'Let's go get the girl.'

* * *

Gade Haggard led Gunn and Pickens in a wide sweep across country that

164

took them several miles to the north before swinging back to the flatter land alongside the river far to the west of Reuben Flack's encampment. The hard ride took a two-hour chunk out of the day, and once they hit the river he and Sam Pickens eased off the trail and allowed their horses to graze while Shako Gunn set about picking up the trail.

Gunn kicked his tireless pinto ahead, then clung to the pommel and leaned low out of the saddle to squint at the hard dirt. Blanket trailing like a dirty, ragged cape, he spent five minutes casting about like a hound dog following a scent.

When he rode back to the others, there was a gleam in his black eyes.

'Could be a beast with eight legs, but I'll settle for two horses, real tight together. One big one, carrying some weight. The other smaller, lighter. They ain't hanging about, Gade.'

'Heading due west?'

'Without a doubt.'

'And we're still ahead of Flack?'

Gunn grinned at Sam Pickens. 'What's the pay for an Injun tracker, Sam?'

'Too doggone much,' Sam said scathingly. 'Why d'you think he's makin' do with a half-blind cavalry sergeant on a beat-up old nag.'

'Yeah, we're still ahead,' Gunn said, chuckling. He slid from the saddle, let his horse wander away with trailing reins, began fashioning a cigarette.

'Slap bang in the middle of two gun-crazies,' Sam Pickens said, dolefully scratching his beard. 'Diamond Jack Sloane up front, Reuben Flack in the rear. Man could get a cricked neck lookin' where he's goin' and watchin' his back.'

'It's exactly where I want to be,' Gade Haggard said. 'Only way Flack can get to Libbie is to ride on through.'

He tossed a canteen to the old ostler, said, 'We'll rest the horses for five minutes, then push on.'

Shako Gunn was sitting in the grass,

greasy hat tipped back, moccasined ankles crossed, eyes narrowed against the acrid smoke from the black cigarette smouldering between his gloved fingers.

'So far, everything's goin' Sloane's way, Gade. He dangled the bait, it's bin took. Now he can stop any time, use that long gun to pop us out of the saddle one by one.'

'I can't argue with that.'

Gunn killed the quirly, caught the canteen tossed by Pickens, climbed to his feet. 'Remember what you were doin' yesterday, Sam?'

The ostler's blue eyes crinkled. 'Sure. Up in the loft keepin' Gade from pluggin' his step-pa — or was it the other way about?'

'Now both of them are, in a manner of speakin', on the same side of the fence. Hatin' each other's guts, but uneasy pardners chasin' after the same gal.' Gunn took a gulp of luke warm water, slapped the stopper into the canteen with his palm and tossed it back to Haggard. 'An' nary a one of 'em,' he finished pointedly, 'knows why.'

'You ready?' Gade said impatiently.

With a shake of his head, Gunn swung into the saddle, put spurs to the pinto, and within seconds all three men were back on the trail and riding west at a steady canter in pursuit of Diamond Jack Sloane.

* * *

To Gade Haggard the remaining hours of daylight drifted past in a blurred confusion of thought. He rode blindly, leaving all the work to his horse. His lean face was set, grey eyes apparently intent on the trail ahead, but inwardly he fretted and fumed and juggled theories in a mind as jumpy as a man with ants in his britches.

They galloped in line abreast across the wide trail, a three man cavalry charge chasing an enemy they couldn't see. And perhaps because he was flanked by the two friends with whom he had spent most of the war years — and was thus mentally transported — as the shadows of sunset crept across the prairie Gade Haggard remembered an incident he had witnessed some years ago when he'd been trudging through the cavalry lines on his way back from the reeking latrines.

The long night before the Confederate victory at the battle of Cedar Mountain, he recalled. Dark, the smell of rain in the air. Officers sprawled around a folding table, drinking rye whiskey outside a sagging, battle-torn tent. Raucous laughter. Battered campaign hats discarded, tight collars unfastened. One man with wild blond hair gleaming in the light of a flickering oil lamp. Reuben Flack. A lieutenant then, bragging drunkenly about a young girl he had ravished many years before in a southern border town.

'Lustrous dark hair,' he rhapsodized, his voice thick with drink. 'The fresh face of a schoolgirl, the ripe body of a woman. Soulful brown eyes, in them a

169

coquettish look'd drive any man wild.
And that I can vouch for, my friends,'
and he'd roared with laughter, told his
now uncomfortable cronies how he had
cajoled then dragged the fifteen-year-
old girl towards an adobe stable, taken
her, whimpering, on straw clogged with
ordure, then hastily pulled up his pants
and left town in a hurry, to ride
north, always north, and always one
water-hole ahead of the girl's enraged
father.

'Made it to the Pecos,' he said, eyes
glassy as he stared at the empty whiskey
bottle, face suddenly contemplative.
'Took me a wife, place called Comanche
Springs . . . '

And a younger, wilder Gade Haggard
had slipped past in the darkness with
hands thrust in his tight waistbelt to
keep them off his pistol, for the rest
of the story he knew and, officer or
no, if he had stayed longer he would
have killed Reuben Flack.

'Emma Sloane,' he whispered now,
recalling Flack's words; and as the

name was whipped away, lost in the warm, dry wind, he swung a wide, sweeping arm to Gunn and Pickens and they slackened their furious pace, pulled off the packed earth of the trail to circle on thick grass and tumble wearily from the blowing horses.

'He's heading for the Staked Plains,' Haggard said hoarsely. 'I figured his game — leastways I figured why he's got it in for Flack.'

'Jesus!' Dust was embedded in the deep lines of Shako Gunn's leathery face. His grey hair was matted his dark eyes bleak. 'Man makes that ride, must have a damn good reason.'

'Flack raped a girl, years ago, on the Mex border. Name of Sloane, so there's your connection with Diamond Jack. Cousin, sister maybe. Flack got away across the Staked Plains. Looks like Jack Sloane's leadin' him back there, figurin' on administerin' a dose of poetic justice.'

'Whatever the hell that is,' Sam Pickens said, feet planted in the grass, arms draped over his saddle.

'He means Sloane ain't gonna plug Flack 'til he gets him out in that goddamn desert,' Shako Gunn said.

'Yeah,' Pickens said drily. 'I figured that, but Gade's choice of words kinda had me fazed.'

'Ain't callin' a halt kinda risky?'

Haggard took a long, searching look back the way they'd come, frowned, said, 'Yeah, Shako, but with half-dead horses we'll not make the plains, never mind git across 'em — and if Sloane's smart enough, he'll take a look at his own horses and reach the same conclusion.'

'All right, so he's some ways ahead, and he rests. But what about Flack?'

'Still some miles back, I reckon. But in any case, you see any cover out there? Any way three men can take us by surprise?'

'Too darned jiggered to look. What I do see is darkness comin' on, Gade, an' I tell you, I got visions of hot chow, coffee, an' warm blankets under the stars.' Gunn reached down, unbuckled the cinch, slid the saddle from his sweating pinto, said, 'I'm old an' I'm tired — and what I say is, if Reuben Flack wants to surprise me, hell, let him go right ahead!'

Gade Haggard chuckled. 'Spoken as one old man to another. OK, we'll bed down by those trees. Sam, you reckon you can get a fire goin'?'

'Not right now, Gade.' The old ostler straightened his wiry frame, dragged himself back into the saddle, swung his horse around so once again he was facing west. 'I got me an itch, an' that's the kind of warning I always give my full attention — only, I don't know whether to scratch my front, or my back. Reckon I'll ride on a coupla miles, ease my mind trouble ain't comin' from that direction.'

Haggard watched Pickens spur his mount away down the trail, listened for a moment to the drum of hooves, then shrugged and walked his horse across to the trees. Shako Gunn joined him, dumped his saddle against one of the gnarled trunks, and while Gade gathered wood he got out utensils and unpacked supplies from his saddle-bags. Before long there was a fire crackling, the flames a welcome blaze beneath the overhanging trees, their brightness dimming the glow of the setting sun and drawing the night in around them.

Blanket draped from his shoulders, Gunn leaned over the fire, hung the blackened coffee pot over the flames, got salt pork sizzling in the pan.

Gade Haggard crossed to his horse, said, 'Right, friend, your turn now,' and stepped back and began to reach down for the cinch buckle.

Something hit him a mighty blow in the shoulder.

He was driven hard against the horse's flank; grunted in shock; heard the blast of the shot, a faint, distant howl of triumph.

Then he was going down, his face sliding across warm leather. He fell on his side, his cheek against the cool grass; and although his eyes were wide open, the camp-fire and the stars were drifting away until nothing was left but the blackness.

* * *

The sound of the shot reached Sam Pickens when he was a mile down the trail, and presented him with a second dilemma.

Just as he'd been puzzled by an itch that wouldn't make up its mind, now he didn't know whether to curse or praise the Lord.

So as he swung his horse in a tight circle, rammed in his heels and rode furiously back up the trail, he did both.

He cursed, because the gunshot told him he'd scratched the wrong itch.

And he praised the Lord, because he knew if he'd been even a hundred yards further on, the shot would have fallen on deaf ears.

As he rode, he dragged his old Hawken from its boot under his right thigh. And this time, he swore, if he got the chance the first bullet would hit Reuben Flack smack between the eyes.

* * *

Another mile due west, the sound of the shot carried so faintly it could have been the snap of a damp, rotten twig, a pine cone falling on a carpet of needles.

Yet it brought Diamond Jack Sloane starting up out of his blanket, black eye staring, one hand slapping for his Dragoon.

It also caught Libbie Ransome on the far side of the shallow pool with a saddle lifted half across her paint's back. As she heard the distant shot, the flurry of movement as Sloane rolled out of his blankets, the snap of his .44 being cocked, she closed her eyes in an agony of despair, let the saddle slip to the ground and pressed her forehead against the horse's warm, pungent hide.

'I guess that little fracas'll sort out the men from the boys, save me a heap of ammunition,' Sloane said happily as a furious rattle of gunfire was carried to them on the night air. 'Time that's over, Flack and Haggard'll likely be the only ones left standing, with no option but to join forces.'

'You're wrong,' Libbie Ransome said softly.

'Mark my words,' Sloane said. 'Now, pick up that saddle and put it where it belongs. We're moving out.

'Oh,' he added, his voice casual, 'and if you try that again — I'll kill you.'

12

The three riders came thundering recklessly across the open prairie in a tight bunch, pistols holstered, coarse faces split by fierce grins, wild rebel yells ringing in the air.

Shako Gunn heard their approach and moved fast.

As the rifle cracked and Gade Haggard grunted in shock he dropped the hot pan and hurled himself away from the fire to melt into the surrounding gloom. He was dragging the battered shotgun from the saddle under the trees even as Haggard fell in a crumpled heap.

As Gunn stuffed shells into his pants pockets his mind was calm, and coldly calculating. He was estimating the odds and, even allowing for the attackers riding in damn near blind, found them daunting.

Then, just as swiftly, he amended that conclusion as his sharp ears picked up the whisper of sound from the west that was Sam Pickens's horse thundering back down the trail. At the same time, his eyes caught the first slow movements from the downed Gade Haggard.

At these encouraging signs he grinned joyously, stepped behind one of the trees, poked the Remington shotgun over a low branch and blasted the first barrel of buckshot in the direction of the approaching riders.

The gun roared. The butt kicked against his shoulder and one of the racing horses screamed and went down in a flurry of dust. The rider tumbled headfirst into the thorny scrub, rolled, came up in a weaving run that took him back behind the dead horse. He flopped down. The barrel of a rifle glinted.

At the shotgun's blast, the other two riders wrenched their horses' heads around and went careering off in

179

opposite directions. Flattened along their horses' backs, they rode hard until they were fifty yards apart, then left their broncs to trot away as they leaped from their saddles and went to ground.

A deep, startled voice yelled, 'Goddamn, she's got a shotgun!'

Using the sound as a target, Shako Gunn blasted the second barrel at what he figured was Reuben Flack. Then he rapidly punched in more shells and took fresh aim while wondering what the hell gave the crazy sonofabitch the idea he was a girl.

He also wondered why there was no answering fire. So far all he'd done was kill a good horse, yet three heavily armed gunmen were cowering in the brush. They'd seen Sam Pickens ride away, shot Gade in the back then launched their attack. Any fool could subtract one from two, so it wouldn't take them long to work out there was just one man left standing.

Why the hell were they waiting?

Then muzzle flame spurted and three quick shots were snapped in the direction of the attackers as the injured Gade Haggard wriggled under the cover of the trees and threw his firepower into the fray.

So now there were two.

Away to the right, another apprehensive voice yelled, 'Rider comin', Major!'

And as Pickens drew closer, suddenly the count was back up to three.

Then a second, more urgent shout from the man with the deep voice made everything clear to Shako Gunn, who listened with amusement as another chipped in angrily to inform the major of his error.

'Ames, Diaz — move in, finish Sloane!'

'Hell, cain't you see you're wrong, Flack!' The words were snarled by the man behind the dead horse. 'Sloane ain't here — this goddamn hornet's nest is Haggard's camp.'

The hidden gunman spat out the last words, then poked his head over the horse's shoulder and began to blaze away with the rifle. From the flanks, Flack and the other man, apprised of their mistake, began a furious barrage of fire with their handguns. For several seconds the gathering dusk was lit by brilliant muzzle flashes. The air was alive with the rattle of pistol fire, the heavier crack of the long gun.

Then, as the firing eased off, died, old Sam Pickens reached the camp. He swung off the trail without slackening pace and came thundering in behind the trees. His wiry body clung recklessly to one side of his horse like a Comanche brave.

His arrival prompted a fresh burst of firing that sent bullets snicking through the branches. Sam yelled in fury as one wild shot plucked at his hat. Then he flung himself from the saddle, slapped his horse on the rump and was alongside Gunn.

'Who's who — and where?' he gasped.

'I reckon that's Ames blastin' with

his rifle from behind the dead hoss. That puts Flack and Diaz on the flanks.'

Without another word, Pickens melted away. Seconds later the heavy boom of his Hawken plains rifle assailed Gunn's eardrums. A burst of profanity issued from where Reuben Flack was lying prone in the scrub. Then the snap of a breaking twig to his right brought Gunn's head around to see Gade Haggard emerge from the gloom, left arm limp, sleeve dark and slick with blood.

'Hell, boy,' Gunn said with feeling, 'for a minute I thought you were a gonner!'

'Yeah, I kinda drifted away for a few seconds.'

Haggard dropped shakily to one knee, placed his .44 on the ground. Then he ripped his bandanna from around his neck, handed it to Gunn, retrieved his pistol and gritted his teeth as the old warhorse ripped the cloth in half, fashioned thick pads which he pressed gently against the bloody wounds on Haggard's shoulder and bound crudely in place with his own bandanna.

Gunfire rattled while Gunn was pulling the knots tight with fingers and teeth. Slugs hummed overhead, socked into a nearby tree. Haggard cursed, loosed two quick shots in return, twisted his head around to squint at Gunn's handiwork.

'Slug went clear through, clean's a whistle,' Shako Gunn said with satisfaction, and Haggard's laugh was rueful.

'My own fool fault,' he said. 'We lost too much time pussyfootin' across country. Sense should've told me once we rejoined the trail Flack'd be breathin' down our necks.'

'Sure fooled Flack,' Gunn said, his voice pained. 'Thought he was up with Sloane, took me for your sister.'

'Just thank your stars it wasn't a big buck Injun all fired up and lookin' for a squaw,' Haggard pointed out with a grim chuckle. Then he ducked back as another fierce fusillade sprayed the encampment with hot, flying lead.

The firing ceased. A sullen silence ensued.

'Flack!' Haggard roared.

'Hell, an' here's me thinkin' Ames had you backshot!'

'This is foolish, Flack. While you and your men're drillin' holes in trees, Jack Sloane's gettin' clear away with Libbie.'

'Nah, he's just keepin' her warm for me.'

Shako Gunn touched Haggard's shoulder, said softly, 'While Flack's talkin', Diaz is workin' his way round on the left.'

'Ain't fifteen-year-old girls more your style, Flack?' Gade Haggard called. Then, hastily he twisted around, followed Gunn's line of sight; thought he saw a shadow shift, way out on the left flank; grinned as, behind them, he caught a glimpse of Sam Pickens's pinned-back hat silhouetted against the night sky as he moved away at a silent, crouching run to meet the new threat.

'You hear me, Flack!'

The answer was a furious burst of fire that sent a withering rain of hot lead smashing into the trees directly in front of them as Ames and Reuben Flack accurately honed in on Haggard's voice.

'For Christ's sake quit jawin', Gade,' Shako Gunn complained.

Then he winced and fell flat as a sharp splinter gouged his cheek. Haggard hit the ground hard, groaned through clenched teeth as his wounded shoulder jarred against a half-buried rock, then pressed himself flat and lay unmoving.

He and Gunn were still down, slugs whistling over their heads from the guns out on the prairie, when a third pistol opened up. Diaz had moved across and around their unprotected left flank. They rolled desperately out of the line of fire as a hail of slugs gouged into the earth inches away, showering them with dirt.

Backed up against a tree, Shako Gunn drew his sixgun and snapped one hasty shot towards Diaz, then quickly put up his gun as the outlaw's fire was answered by the heavy boom of the Hawken.

Sam Pickens, fearless as ever, had located the target.

There was a sudden furious thrashing as Diaz blundered through the brush. Again the heavy Hawken blasted. But this time Pickens had been hasty — and he was answered by four measured shots from Diaz, aimed at the Hawken's muzzle flash.

For an instant there was a heavy silence. Then Gunn and Haggard heard a low, half-stifled groan of agony, followed by the crackle of branches breaking under a falling body.

As if at a signal, all shooting ceased.

'Hey, Major,' Diaz called cheerfully, his voice drifting eerily out of the darkness. 'That skinny old ostler, I reckon he's smashed his last window this side of Hades.'

'Jesus Christ almighty!' Shako Gunn said, his voice choked with fury.

'They're closing in,' Gade Haggard said grimly.

In the fading light, he caught the glint of the Winchester as Ames emerged from behind his dead horse. At the same time there was a low whistle far out to the right. Seconds later Haggard heard the jingle of a bridle as Reuben Flack remounted.

'Flack's all mouth,' Gade murmured, voice tight with pain. 'He'll hang back, the mighty general directin' his troops.'

Metal scraped as Gunn fed shells into the Remington.

'So we sit tight.' His teeth gleamed white in the gloom. 'Since you last yelled, they've sprayed these trees with slugs. After that, not a peep from you or me. Far as Ames and Diaz know, we're both dead.'

'I see Ames,' Haggard said. 'Thirty yards, comin' in fast.'

'I'll take Diaz — when I kin see the

murdering bastard!'

Gunn closed the shotgun. The click was barely audible. But instantly Diaz's gun blasted from behind them. Sparks flew as the slug slammed into the shotgun's double barrel. It whined away into the darkness. The shotgun flew from Gunn's nerveless fingers.

Then Ames opened up with the Winchester. Gade hugged the dirt, pinned down by the accurate fire. Ames came pounding across the short grass at a jinking run. He was working the Winchester's lever like a madman as he fired from the hip.

Gunn was cursing, trying to shake feeling back into numbed fingers. The shotgun was six feet away, and useless. He fumbled for his pistol. His teeth were bared in a snarl as he listened to Diaz crashing through the bushes.

The .45 came out of its holster — only to slip from his clumsily grasping hand and bounce off his moccasined foot.

189

Ames was now less than twenty feet away, beyond the trees but closing on the camp-fire. His lean face was wild in the light of the flames. Again his right hand worked the rifle's lever, squeezed the trigger.

There was a hollow click as the Winchester's hammer fell on an empty chamber.

Ames howled his frustration. He hurled the rifle away from him. His hand went down, slapped leather, came up with his sixgun. He leaped through the flames and smoke.

Coolly, Gade Haggard took a careful bead and shot him between the eyes.

Ames flew backwards, dead on his feet. Haggard twisted painfully to face the charging Diaz. Muzzle flashes lit up the trees, the scuffed earth. He saw Shako Gunn down on his knees. His hand was reaching for the sixgun that lay half buried in dead leaves. The shotgun was lying alongside a rock. Both barrels were dented, the scarred metal gleaming.

As Gunn's fingers touched the six-gun, Haggard rolled, came up on his knees. Then Diaz began shooting. A slug clipped Haggard's boot. Another wild shot whined past his ear. It buried itself in the camp-fire. Blazing branches cartwheeled in a shower of sparks.

Then Diaz burst from the scrub. Shako Gunn saw him coming, abandoned the sixgun. He scrambled away from the trees and grabbed the useless shotgun, grasping it by the barrel. His numb fingers curled around the hot metal.

Diaz was almost on him. His dark eyes were wild, black moustache bristling over gleaming white teeth. He loosed one wild shot. It sang harmlessly towards the sky. He braced himself, fired again.

The slug raised a gout of earth between Gunn's legs as he came up with the shotgun in both hands. He pivoted fast, used his body movement to swing the gun in a wide, powerful sweep.

Again Diaz fired. The slug seared

along Gunn's ribs like a red-hot iron. He sucked in a breath. Anger roared from his gaping mouth as he directed all his strength into his shoulders and arms, into the shotgun he was wielding like a long club.

The flailing butt was a blur of movement. It struck Diaz on the side of the head with the sound of a sharp axe-blade biting into a log. The gunman was knocked off his feet. He flopped sideways, hit the ground as limp as empty sack. Blood gushed from his ear. His eyes stared sightlessly at the night skies.

Shako Gunn leaned forward from the waist. His legs were braced as he rested his weight on the shotgun. Then he straightened, spat, threw the shattered weapon down by the dead gunman. He turned. Haggard was on his knees, the hand still holding his .44 pressed tight against his injured shoulder.

As the first pale light of the rising moon reached the clearing, Gade Haggard saw that Gunn's face was streaked with blood, his shirt blood-soaked. His blanket was a filthy rag trailing in the dust. For a long minute he stared at his old friend; saw the lined, leathery face crack in a grin.

'You figure on stayin' there all night?' Shako Gunn queried.

'Ain't no reason for me to move,' Haggard said. 'Reckon I'll just sit back, watch you wipe out the whole goddamn outlaw breed with that broken shotgun.'

'I'll settle for Reuben Flack,' Gunn said, his eyes suddenly hard.

'Well, he's out there somewhere,' Haggard said. He stretched out his hand and Gunn grasped it, pulled him to his feet. Then, as Gunn stooped to retrieve his pistol and Haggard turned towards the smouldering embers of the scattered fire, saddle leather creaked, and there was the oily click of a gun cocking.

'Stay very still,' Reuben Flack said out of the darkness.

Gunn was already stooping. He

continued on down, scooped up his .45 on the way and rolled out of sight behind the trees.

Flack's laugh was uneasy.

'I can see Ames over by the campfire. Where's Diaz?'

'For Christ's sake!' Haggard swore. 'Put up your gun and ride in. We need to talk.'

'You think I'm crazy? There's nothing to say, nothing to stop me putting a bullet in you right now, Haggard, then riding after Sloane.'

'In answer to your question,' Shako Gunn growled, 'sure you're crazy, Major. Crazy to think that gal Libbie's gonna take a shine to you. Crazy not to plug Gade when you had the chance back in Desolation. And sure as hell you're crazy to think you can do it when Sam Pickens's got that Hawken lined up on your backbone.'

For long, tense moments, Haggard sensed Reuben Flack chewing over Gunn's words. The wily cavalryman was telling himself his old sergeant was bluffing — but there was no way he could prove it. Without Pickens, he held all the aces. Mounted on a fast horse, shooting from darkness into a clearing that was now bathed in cold light, Haggard, a standing, helpless target, Shako Gunn down behind the trees and aiming blind at shadows — he surely fancied his chances.

But raw courage was not just Reuben Flack's weak suit — it had rarely been present in any deck he dealt! Abruptly, Haggard heard the quieter click of a pistol's hammer being lowered, twigs snapped under a horse's hooves, and stiff branches were roughly brushed aside as Flack rode through, head ducked, fancy sixgun back in its holster.

He drew rein, slid from the saddle as Shako Gunn stepped out into the open, sixgun held down alongside his thigh.

'Now listen close,' Gade Haggard said. He pouched his .44, reached into his bloody shirt pocket, found his tobacco sack and tossed it to Gunn. 'Your men are dead, Flack — yeah, and so's Sam Pickens.'

He smiled mirthlessly as Flack spat a curse, held up his hand, went on, 'We could stand jawin' all night, but that's time wasted. So here's the way I see it. Flack, you could've lit out once you saw Diaz and Ames were outgunned. One of the reasons you didn't is because that'd mean facing Diamond Jack Sloane — and you're no gunman.'

'Ain't no man at all,' Shako Gunn said, busy fashioning a cigarette.

Flack's jaw whitened. 'You were army, Sergeant. Only a fool rides in blind, against superior fire-power.'

'As we've just witnessed.' Gunn laughed, handed the thin black cigarette to Haggard, struck a match. 'But a goddamn Sharps Buff? Hell, if the man's relyin' on that, he's the fool. Easy enough pickin' off a sittin' duck. You ever tried lookin' through a 'scope at a distant target that's hoppin' about like spit on a hot tin plate?'

In the flare of the match, Flack's face was haunted. He watched Haggard blow a jet of smoke, said, 'All right — what's the other reason I didn't ride on?'

'Because a while back I mentioned a fifteen-year-old girl,' Haggard said. 'That scratched a painful sore. You think you know now what Sloane holds against you.'

'You and me both,' Reuben Flack said, and there was biting cynicism in his sharp glance.

'All right.' Haggard nodded, felt the stir of an uneasy foreboding as he looked into the cold blue eyes. He said, 'A long time ago a man followed you into the Staked Plains. Seems he was half crazy, out to kill you for what you did to his innocent young daughter. Has to be too long ago for that father to've been Diamond Jack. So I reckon Jack's her brother.'

'Whiskey loosens a man's tongue,' Flack said, nodding wearily. 'Yeah, I was young and hot blooded. If it wore skirts, I chased it. If it wore pants and toted a gun, often as not I deliberately goaded it into a sixgun showdown.' He glowered at a grinning, disbelieving Shako Gunn, went on, 'You were no different, Haggard. You were a kid when I reached Comanche Springs, but after you left home you grew up fast, had an eye for pretty girls, were happy to get involved in gunfights — only, in one of them, something went wrong and you killed a young boy.'

'Let me guess,' Shako Gunn said scornfully. 'That boy was Diamond Jack Sloane's brother.'

'His son. I offered him cash to kill Haggard, he told me the story. Why would he lie? Since that hot day in San Miguel, he's been on Haggard's trail. The war was an irritating hiccup. Then, coupla days ago, he got lucky.'

Haggard flicked the cigarette towards the dying camp-fire, eased himself painfully erect, testing his left shoulder.

'I rode into a good many towns, in

my time,' he said reflectively. 'But I was never in San Miguel.'

Flack laughed derisively. 'Sure. A man accuses you of killing a kid, what the hell else could you say?' he scoffed.

'Sloane thinks I shot his son, he's been hunting the wrong man,' Haggard declared. 'And I'll tell him that to his face.'

'Seems I heard similar honourable but misguided words in Desolation,' Gunn said drily. 'You set out to look in Flack's eyes, find out what makes him tick, ended up in a nest of rattlers. But, hell,' he said, 'I know you'll take no goddamn notice of me . . . '

He stomped away through the trees, noisily gathered together the cooking utensils from the ruins of the fire, stowed them in his saddle-bags then lugged the heavy rig over to his horse.

By the time he'd saddled his own horse, then Haggard's, the others had dragged the three bodies into the clearing and Flack had begun hacking out the shallow graves.

While Haggard watched and fretted it took Gunn and Flack another thirty minutes to complete the job. Then, filthy, glistening with sweat, they stood back and removed their hats while Gade Haggard gruffly said a few words over the three graves.

That done, the three men mounted up and prepared to leave.

It had been in Gade Haggard's mind to leave Reuben Flack behind. Those sentiments had been echoed by Shako Gunn.

'Leave the bastard,' he'd murmured. 'Take his horse and his boots, let him walk barefoot.'

But for Gade Haggard, the issues involved were more complex.

In one way or another the ghost of Reuben Flack had been haunting him for too many long, bitter years; had first weighed down his young shoulders as he rode south to the Mex border; had harried and mocked him through a brutal war and, with the return of peace, would have had him killed if the gunman Flack had bought with gold had not turned out to be a maverick with his own massive grievance.

Setting Flack loose in the desert would not lay that ghost.

In addition, Haggard knew that Reuben Flack had crossed his own personal Rubicon the day he raped a young girl, fled into the Staked Plains and rode on to Comanche Springs. If there was any symbolism in that act, then in that burning desert heat Flack had left behind his own private Hell.

Diamond Jack Sloane was calling him back for the reckoning, and Gade Haggard saw no reason to stand in his way.

★ ★ ★

The moon had climbed high while they buried their dead. When they rode away from the stand of trees they left behind them in the clearing three graves and the moon-cast shadows of their crude wooden crosses.

On one of those crosses there rested a battered hat, its brim still pinned back by a broken thorn.

Haggard led the way onto the trail, riding painfully askew in the saddle, his body swaying awkwardly to his horse's gait. He was acutely aware of his weakness, shocked by Flack's revelation about Jack Sloane's son, at a loss to know how he was going to get close to Sloane while the gunman held Libbie hostage.

Behind him, Reuben Flack rode stiffly erect, but there was a sickness in his stomach at the thought of what lay ahead. Ames and Diaz, the tough gunslingers he had relied on, were dead. And he kept seeing the menacing, black-clad figure of Diamond Jack Sloane, the single, glittering eye of the man who, by his own statement, had hate enough to spare.

As if Sloane wasn't handful enough, there was also Gade Haggard. Flack had robbed and deserted the man's mother, hanged his brothers, had always lusted after his sister. More than enough reason for a man to want him dead. And as he rode with his thoughts, his shoulders cringed because behind him rode Shako Gunn, dark eyes glinting in the light of the moon, blanket swept back to clear his holster.

From the head of the line, as he raised a hand to indicate that he was increasing the pace to an economical, ground-eating canter, Gade Haggard turned stiffly in the saddle.

In Flack's drawn face, in the eyes that were pale in the darkness, he saw weakness and uncertainty, the turmoil of his thinking; it was the face of a man who sensed that in the next few hours he would be made, or broken.

Haggard shifted his gaze to the leathery features of Shako Gunn, the glow of his black cigarette, the buccaneering sweep of the blanket; the greasy hat shading the black eyes that glittered with strength and life.

One of Gunn's gloved hands rested on the pommel for, led by a slack trail rope, Sam Pickens's horse was bringing up the rear. The stirrups were tied. The old man's boots, linked with a rawhide thong, hung across the saddle. From the saddle scabbard, its butt glossy in the moonlight, there jutted the old ostler's Hawken plains rifle.

And because it reminded him of his first sight of Diamond Jack Sloane as the man in black had ridden out of Desolation with the deadly Sharps Buffalo shining in the late evening sunshine, Sam Pickens's rifle was in Haggard's thoughts throughout that long night.

13

In the bright morning sunlight, the hundred-foot-high bluffs and buttresses edging the Staked Plains loomed as an awesome barrier. From a short way up the first distant slopes, the rocky canyons and ravines serrating the heights appeared as inhospitable areas of deep shadow in which, it seemed, even the nimblest of horses would find no foothold.

'Joe Loving went up by a different route, took a herd of longhorns across that wasteland,' Libbie said softly, her eyes on the shimmering crest. 'A lot of steers died, but what Joe told us about Texas was inspiring. We used his trail, Mil Ransome and I, rode across from the Pecos then down from the dry uplands to make our home on the Concho — and then you came, and in a few seconds of violence wiped out everything I held dear.'

Diamond Jack Sloane made no answer. Yet as he surveyed the escarpments through field-glasses, he knew that the girl was right: the difficulties of the ascent were illusory; the slopes were long and gradual; the canyons softly grassed; the higher ground gradually becoming grittier and more rock-strewn.

An hour's hard ride would see them at the crest. Over that lay the white, searing landscape he had chosen for the reckoning with the soldier who had destroyed his family, the renegade who had killed his son.

'You'll never make it,' Libbie Haggard said, her face triumphant, and Sloane shot a baleful glance at the girl, at the lame, lathered pony that had slowed the night ride. Then he turned in the saddle to sweep the glasses across their back trail.

Three riders. One spare horse. No more than four miles back.

They were still swiftly closing the

gap. At dawn, when he first spotted them, they were dots on the horizon. He had looked back three times since then. The second time he recognized them for what they were. Each time since then, without appearing to have moved, they had been closer.

'Was six of 'em when they set out,' he said, and laughed harshly, remembering the sunset sounds of gunfire.

'And now three will run you down,' she said, swinging out of the saddle to stoop and massage the paint's trembling foreleg.

'You're wrong. I'll face them on ground of my choosing. And you're wasting time.' He put away the field-glasses, waited impatiently while she drank from her canteen and remounted. Then, with a final glance at the pursuing riders, he touched the big bay with his heels, said, 'Get that crippled cayuse moving,' and led the way at a fast trot up the gradually increasing slopes.

They progressed without trouble for

thirty minutes, with nothing to be heard but the creak of leather, the snorts of the horses, the ring of metal shoes on rock. The trail rope stretched tight as a fiddle string from Sloane's saddle as the bay used its powerful muscles to draw the flagging pony along. But the paint's lame foreleg was making its gait uneven, the regular, fierce jerks on the rope sapping the bigger animal's strength.

Sloane fretted and fumed, knowing that while they were labouring up the difficult slopes, the men pursuing him were racing across the flat, open plain.

They would be closing fast.

The dazzling orb of the sun rose quickly. As they climbed higher, the heat grew more intense, became an oppressive weight beating down on them from cloudless blue skies. The last of the grass was left behind. On the hard, stony ground, both horses slowed and began to blow. Sloane's black hair was slick with sweat, his clothing coated with fine white dust. Astride the following horse, Libbie had lifted her bandanna to cover her mouth. Her eyes were red-rimmed.

Diamond Jack Sloane glanced back more frequently. He no longer needed his field glasses. The chasing group were still crossing the flat grasslands. Sloane watched them draw nearer. And as Libbie's lame pony became almost a dead weight at the end of the rope, his lips drew back from his teeth in a snarl of impotent fury.

They negotiated a steep incline where the trail crossed slabs of flat rock riven by wide, shallow fissures. Twenty yards ahead it skirted a massive, jagged boulder behind which the ground fell away steeply.

Sloane's bay whinnied nervously, tossing its head as it picked its way across the uneven slabs. It drew level with the boulder, edged past, urged on by a tight-lipped Diamond Jack Sloane. Its eyes were white with fright, yet it was still moving, still sure-footed.

But, suddenly, the dragging weight of

the struggling pony was its undoing.

As the big lead horse passed the huge boulder, one metal shoe skidded on smooth rock, causing a foreleg to slide into a wide crack in the rocky trail. The horse lurched, squealed its fright, regained its balance and took several skittish steps to the side.

Jack Sloane cursed, fighting to stay in the saddle. He felt the trail rope go slack as the big horse backed up. Sensing relief, Libbie's exhausted pony tossed its head and turned painfully until it was facing back down the slope. As Libbie leaned forward, whispering soothing words, patting its glistening neck, its nostrils flared and it made as if to bound down the hill.

At once, the trail rope snapped taut.

With a shrill cry, Libbie was thrown forwards out of the saddle. She hit the rocky ground at the side of the boulder with a bone-jarring thump, flopped over the edge of the trail and slithered on her face down a loose scree slope.

Instantly, Jack Sloane was out of the saddle and sliding the big Sharps from its scabbard. His blunt thumb eased back the hammer as he stepped swiftly and easily across the flat rock like a big cat. From the shadows alongside the towering boulder his eye quartered the slope below him, settled on the bouncing rocks, the haze of dust shimmering in the sunlight, the tumbling, sliding figure of Libbie Ransome.

Then the rifle was at his shoulder.

Sloane squinted along the sights, picked up the slithering figure, stayed with it, squeezed the trigger. The blast echoed from the high rocks. The shot winged wide. Far below now, the girl reached the edge of the scree, regained her feet and broke into a stumbling run.

There was nowhere for her to go. Away from the rocks, she was on grassy slopes that afforded no cover.

As he weighed up the situation, Diamond Jack Sloane's thin lips twisted into a cruel grin.

The girl was his hole card, the bait he trailed before his hunters like a trembling deer displayed to draw in the circling wolves. Alive and running free, she was of no use to him. But dead, her slim young body blasted apart by a single shot from the powerful buffalo gun, she would again be a potent force. They would take one look at her, lying in a pool of dark blood, and follow him clear to Hell.

Moving with the speed of long practice, Sloane reloaded the Sharps. Then he sank to one knee, pulled the big gun into his shoulder, and took steady, careful aim.

* * *

'Either of you any good with that Hawken?'

'Could hit those high cliffs without tryin',' Shako Gunn said. 'But don't ask me where.'

'Just let me get close, with a pistol,'

Reuben Flack snarled, his chest swelling with bravado.

Some 500 yards from the unexpected explosion of violence they had reined in at the echoes of the first booming shot, close enough now to see with the naked eye the two horses on the steep track, the sunlight flashing on the barrel of the Sharps, the puff of smoke as Diamond Jack Sloane fired from the cover of the big boulder.

Some hundred feet below him, miraculously unharmed after the hair-raising tumble down the loose scree, Libbie Ransome was on her feet and running.

As they watched, a puff of dust erupted from the ground close to her racing feet. She jerked as if hit, her stride faltered, and they caught the flash of sunlight on her white face as she frantically looked right and left for cover.

Then she had recovered her poise. And now she began swerving as she ran, in a brave attempt to avoid the hot lead.

'The gully, get in the gully,' Gade Haggard breathed tensely. 'Run to your right, girl.'

'Cain't see it from where she is,' Gunn said.

'He'll get her, next shot,' said Reuben Flack.

'Maybe,' Haggard gritted. 'But remember what Gunn told you about spit on a hot tin plate? She's a fast moving target — '

'Not any more, she ain't,' Gunn cut in, as a second shot from the Sharps reverberated through the hot air and Libbie Ransome's right leg buckled. She hit the ground hard, and lay in a still, crumpled heap.

'Let's go!'

Mouthing a curse, Gade Haggard dug in his spurs and urged his horse into a furious gallop. He leaned forward, favouring his painful, wounded shoulder as he stretched out along his straining mount's neck. Peering ahead, he was aware of the thunder of pounding hooves as Gunn's tough, ragged pinto drew alongside. Through narrowed eyes he saw the dark shape on the grassy slopes move, unfold, become recognizable. The girl had climbed to her feet. When she again broke into a stumbling run she was limping badly. But now she was moving towards the unseen gully.

'She'll make it!' Shako Gunn cried. 'Sloane's backed off!'

This was a roar of triumph from Reuben Flack, swiftly drawing level then pulling away from them as his big horse's long stride ate up the ground.

As Libbie Ransome's stumbling run at last brought her to the gully and she slid out of sight, a relieved Gade Haggard lifted his gaze and saw that Flack was right.

From his high vantage point, Sloane had judged accurately that this phase of the cruel game he played was over. He could not find the right angle to kill the girl huddled in the deep gully. If he hung about too long, he was putting himself in danger.

Already, he was cutting it fine.

Ahead, Flack was urging his horse up the first slopes, with Haggard and Gunn close behind.

High above them, Diamond Jack Sloane used his knife to slash the taut trail rope. As the lame pony lurched away and began to hobble down the track, Sloane mounted the big bay and began the short, steep ride that would take him over the crest and on to the sun-baked expanse of the Staked Plains.

'Flack'll maybe get what he wanted,' Gunn called breathlessly. 'Be within pistol shot pretty soon.'

But even as he spoke and Haggard flashed a knowing, derisive grin, the major had pulled his horse off the trail and was making for the gully. He reached it, slid from his still moving horse, stumbled towards the spot where the girl had disappeared.

'We let him go?'

'Sloane?' Reluctantly slackening the pace, Haggard nodded. 'Sure. Hitting

Libbie with that gun was always going to be difficult. Picking us off the trail, one by one, would be like pluggin' those sittin' ducks.' Then they were both alongside the shallow ravine, and dismounting to witness another drama as Libbie Ransome clawed her way up its loose, sloping sides, struggling furiously to pull away from Reuben Flack's grasp.

'Shako,' she gasped, 'get this monster off me before I scratch out his eyes.'

At once, Reuben Flack released his hold. Awkwardly, Libbie stepped away, breathing hard, breasts rising and falling beneath the dust-caked cotton shirt.

'Shako?' Haggard echoed, his face puzzled.

'Guess you're the only man in Texas don't know that, for a while there before the war, I was your ma's foreman,' Gunn said somewhat sheepishly. But already his words were wasted, the question they answered forgotten. Gade Haggard had moved across to the girl and was standing hesitantly before her, his eyes hungrily searching the pale, scratched face.

'It's been a long time,' he said huskily. 'No freckles, no pigtails, but I'd know those eyes anywhere, Libbie.'

'And I yours,' she said softly. Her eyes left his face, took in his tall, angular frame, the shirt stained and stiffened with dried blood.

'Oh, Gade,' she moaned, 'why, why did you stay away?' With a little exclamation of chagrin that changed swiftly to a soft sigh of pleasure she slipped into his arms, burying her face against his chest as his hands lifted to stroke her damp hair.

For a few seconds they remained like that, the only sounds their breathing, the jingle of bridles as the horses grazed, the faint rattle of hooves and falling rock from high up the trail.

Then, as if those jarring sounds finally broke through the intense emotion of the meeting, Gade Haggard stepped back. Hands grasping her shoulders, he said harshly, 'Diamond Jack Sloane. Did he harm you in any way? Your leg . . . ?'

'No, Gade, nothing. He has kept well away from me on the trail. That one bullet snapped off the heel of my boot. But before my eyes he murdered my husband and our dear old wrangler. That crime will haunt me for as long as I live.'

Then she frowned. 'But you, Gade, and . . . ' She turned to glare at Reuben Flack, her gaze contemptuous, then looked anxiously into Haggard's face. 'He told me that you have done wicked things, both of you, and that was why he took me. I was the bait. He knew you'd follow, he *wanted* you to follow — '

'He's lying,' Flack blustered. 'You know me better'n that, Libbie — '

'About Gade, I'm sure he lies — but I know you well enough to believe him,' she snapped.

'No matter,' Haggard said. 'From now on we're after him for the crime

219

he committed — and right now he's getting away.'

'With my gold,' Flack blurted.

'Which you gave to him as payment for killing my brother,' Libbie reminded scathingly.

'Hold up there,' Shako Gunn said laconically. 'Seems to me we're busy chasin' our tails up a box canyon, circlin' around what was and what might have been 'stead of figurin' what to do about that feller up ahead.'

'Only one thing to do,' Gade Haggard said. As he looked at Libbie, at the ageing Reuben Flack, the ageless Shako Gunn, he saw in their eyes their mute acknowledgement. The problems posed by Diamond Jack Sloane would not go away.

'We could ride away from here,' he said quietly. 'But sometime, some-where, Sloane would come back at us.'

'Isn't it worth taking that chance?' Libbie said, her eyes imploring as she looked from her brother to Shako

Gunn. 'Sloane murdered my husband, but for the sake of peace I'm willing to turn away.' Despite the heat, she shivered. 'I've been close to the man. He's obsessed. If you go after him he's sure to kill one of you — and you, Shako, you know that more than anything in the world, Ma wants her son back home.'

'Which brings us up against the same problem,' Gade Haggard said grimly. 'From here, there's only one way home,' and he nodded towards the jagged crest, the vast, unseen plains. 'Sloane's not getting away. He's up there, waiting for us.'

That knowledge gave Haggard breathing space; the time to gather again the strength that had leaked out of him with his blood, the resolve to push on.

Watching him, knowing that the decision would be made later, Shako Gunn moved away to gather wood and build a fire at the end of the gully. Soon, the stifling, uneasy silence was broken by the clatter of pots and pans, and presently the four of them were filling empty bellies with hot coffee and fresh biscuits as the sun climbed to its zenith and the heat beat down.

Replete, they settled back against the hot rocks. Libbie sat in silence, her back turned stiffly to avoid the probing eyes of Reuben Flack. Shako Gunn fashioned one of his black cigarettes, smoked lazily, eyes slitted against the sun.

Gade Haggard declined the offer of Gunn's tobacco with a bleak smile, then climbed to his feet. He crossed the grass to the ground-tethered broncs, slid his Winchester from its saddle boot, then remembered his useless shoulder and reluctantly pushed it back. Loosening his sixgun, he started up the track.

Several minutes after his footsteps had faded, from high up the trail near the massive boulder they heard a faint whinny, a single shot.

When Haggard returned, he was carrying Libbie's saddle over his good right arm. His face was hard, his jaw set as he dumped the saddle on the grass.

'Your pony's leg was a mess,' he told Libbie bluntly. 'From now on you ride Sam Pickens's horse.' Then, eyes steely, he said, 'Shako, this is not your fight. You hang well back with Libbie. The major wants his gold. We'll ride after Sloane together, get this thing finished.'

Still lazily smoking, Gunn said, 'You, ride with Flack? Hell, I never thought I'd see the day.'

'Makes sense,' Flack said, climbing to his feet. 'Out there on the plains there ain't no way Sloane can gun down two of us.'

'A word of advice, Gade,' Shako Gunn warned. 'Watch your back.'

'Sure,' Haggard said. 'With me, Flack'll be where I can see him — and well away from Libbie.'

He found a stirrup and stepped awkwardly into the saddle. Aware of Libbie standing with clenched fists, he wheeled the horse, waited for Reuben

Flack to mount up, then turned his face towards her.

'Maybe we'll talk Sloane around,' he said lamely. 'Make him see sense.' Then, unexpectedly, the look of despair on her white, strained face was like a knife being twisted in his heart. He swallowed, shrugged helplessly. 'Maybe not. But one way or another, Sis, this'll be over by sundown,' and without thinking he swung away, put spurs to his horse and started it up the steep, rocky trail.

It was several moments before he heard the rattle of hooves, and realized that despite Shako Gunn's warning, Reuben Flack was now behind him.

★ ★ ★

Unaware that his pursuers were hesitating on the lower slopes of the escarpment, Diamond Jack Sloane crossed the ridge at noon and spurred his mount cruelly into the barren wasteland of the Staked Plains.

As he rode down the long slopes leading off the rise, the sky was transformed from deep blue to a blazing white. The heat was blistering. For half a mile or so there was a scattering of parched sage. Then even that was left behind and the rattle of the horse's hooves was muffled by the thin blanket of white alkali dust that covered the rocky ground for as far as the eye could see. When disturbed, it rose in a fine, drifting cloud. After a mile, Sloane's black attire was coated with the dust, his single, red-rimmed eye squinting ahead out of a white mask.

He rode hard for an hour, from time to time passing the bleached, flesh-stripped skeletons of longhorn cattle that had perished on the long drive to the Pecos. At such times his mouth would tighten, the hatred in his black eye become a fierce blaze of fire. For, in his mind, those bones were the bones of his father and, unbidden, his head would twist to look back for a sign of the men who rode behind.

Eventually, he was forced to slacken the pace as in the intense heat the big horse began to falter. They had covered many miles. Now Sloane became acutely aware of his surroundings. He kept a constant watch for shallow arroyos, for small outcrops of rock; for any relief in the monotonous, white flatness that could be used for cover.

Diamond Jack Sloane had from the start put his reliance on the powerful Sharps Buffalo. He had chosen the Staked Plains for the reckoning because of their agonizing associations with his past — and because he knew that nobody could pursue him without themselves being dangerously exposed.

In a short time, his diligence bore fruit.

On the far side of a small, glittering salt flat, a wedge of rock poked through the dust. Fifty yards long. Nowhere more than six feet high.

Eagerly, Sloane circled around it like a cagey wolf, eyed it critically from all angles, dismounted with deep satisfaction. Then, because he knew that without his horse he was a dead man, he poured warm water from his canteen into his dust-caked black hat, and let the weary animal dip its head and take the edge off its thirst.

Only then did he slip the big rifle from its scabbard, take his field-glasses from the saddle-bag, and settle down to search the far horizon from the cover of rocks that were too hot to touch.

At first, peering through the powerful glasses was like staring directly into the white-hot heart of a furnace. Then, as his watering eye grew accustomed to the dazzling glare, he began to distinguish shapes: the jagged outline of the ridge he had crossed more than an hour ago, shimmering in the heat; the dark, apparently motionless speck that was a single rider.

One man?

Diamond Jack Sloane dragged his sleeve across his lips, reached up to ease the black patch away from the sweating skin of his empty eye socket.

First six, then three — now one.

Or maybe not. There was more than one way up a cliff. So one of them had followed his trail, the others were riding north to come up on his left flank.

Then, figuring that in any case he had most of an hour to wait, Jack Sloane sat down in the dust, turned his back to the searing rock and began to prepare the big Sharps.

14

Three hundred yards after cresting the rise, Reuben Flack shot Gade Haggard in the back.

He did it from thirty yards away, watched with a savage grin as Haggard toppled from his saddle and lay face down in the white dust. Then, keeping his sixgun cocked and ready, Flack rode forward to gaze at the crumpled figure.

The back of Haggard's shirt was soaked with fresh blood. Too much, Flack figured, to have seeped from the old wound. Too much, also, for him to detect a fresh bullet hole. A second bullet would finish the job.

His finger was tightening on the trigger when he heard a roar of anger from the rise behind him. The crack of a sixgun, the whine of a slug passing close to his head, were followed by the rapid drum of approaching hooves.

Swiftly holstering his Colt, Flack put spurs to his horse and urged it out across the searing dust of the Staked Plains.

For a mile he rode like a madman, sharp spurs raking the horse's flanks, the image of the dark shape lying in the dust telling him that Gade Haggard was dead, that nothing now stood between him and the girl he had lusted after for more than fifteen long years.

Somewhere ahead there waited a gunslinger who had sworn to kill him. But now it was just the two of them, man against man. The flat landscape afforded no hiding place. They were equals, neither man having the advantage.

Diamond Jack Sloane carried a powerful gun, and had proved he could handle it with skill. But the shimmering air dancing above the baked surface of the Staked Plains would make accurate aiming a matter of luck, the trajectory of the slug erratic. Sloane's only advantage was based on the extra range of the Sharps. If his first shot went wild, Flack would be close enough to use his Winchester to deadly effect.

But, as he slackened his headlong pace and began to follow the tracks that arrowed straight and true into the heart of the desert, there was time for thinking. A certain clarity comes to a man's thoughts when he faces the possibility of his own death. And so, perhaps for the first time, two facts became clear to Reuben Flack.

The first was that by murdering Gade Haggard in cold blood he had not removed an obstacle that cleared the way to Libbie Ransome, but had created a far greater one that put her beyond his reach for all time. Far from infuriating him, he realized, the knowledge brought with it a feeling of immense relief.

The second fact was much less complicated. A man had duped him out of a large quantity of gold. That man was Diamond Jack Sloane and, eyes narrowed against the blinding glare, Flack swore that it would take more than a one-eyed gunslinger with a fancy rifle to cheat Major Reuben Flack out of a leather pouch full of gold eagles that was rightfully his.

And then he chuckled.

Rightfully his, that was, since the night he took the last, substantial Confederate cavalry payroll of the war into his safekeeping and made off with it into the darkness.

* * *

Shako Gunn reached him first. The ragged pinto was still back on its haunches sliding stiff-legged in the dust when Gunn kicked his moccasins free of the stirrups and hit the ground running.

He dropped to his knees beside the still figure, took hold of the right shoulder, eased Haggard over onto his back.

Two keen grey eyes looked up at him.

'Easy, Shako,' Haggard said softly. 'If Flack looks over his shoulder, I want him to see what he expects to see.'

Shako Gunn drew a shuddering breath of relief. 'And that is?'

'The dead body of Gade Haggard, being toted back the way he came — belly-down over his saddle.'

'Libbie's watchin' back there. She's seen her husband murdered, spent a day and night with his killer. You think that girl can stand another shock?'

'When she see's what's goin' on she'll put spurs to Sam's horse and ride over here to help. You'd expect that. So will Flack. If he's watching, he'll be convinced.'

Gunn looked at the dried blood stiffening Haggard's shirt front, said, 'You hit agin?'

Haggard chuckled, shook his head. 'No. He's gettin' old and careless. I fell awkward, made sure the old wound took a knock when I hit the dirt then rolled over so he could see some fresh blood.'

'You was still lucky,' Gunn gritted. 'An' right now you'd best brace yourself because you've got me riled and I'm about to do something real convincing.'

He stood up, took hold of Haggard's booted feet and dragged him unceremoniously the twenty yards through the dust to the jittery roan. Then, with Reuben Flack now no more than a dark speck in the dust cloud drifting across the featureless plains, he murmured soothing words to the snorting horse while he struggled to boost Haggard's considerable weight upright.

'Throw your goddamn arms over,' he panted, hip and shoulder braced against the sagging figure. 'Flack's halfway to hell and I'm a tired old man.'

Using his good right arm, wincing as the skin across his shoulders pulled tight threatening to rip his wounds wide open, Haggard helped Gunn ease him up so he was folded belly-down across the saddle. Settled there, by twisting his head he was able to locate the disappearing dust cloud, then turn the other way and watch Gunn mount the waiting pinto.

Seconds later, Gunn had collected the trailing reins of Haggard's roan and was leading the animal with its gruesome burden back towards the ridge.

Libbie Ransome met them halfway.

She was crying.

★ ★ ★

As the sun went down and the flaring red banners of sunset streamed across the western skies, they built a fire on the lee slopes of the ridge and Shako Gunn brewed fresh coffee.

Hunkered down, tin mugs clutched in their hands, they ruminated on a situation created by Diamond Jack Sloane that seemed to leave him holding a handful of aces.

'I ain't heard no shots,' Gunn said, a grim, blanket-draped figure sitting with his back against a rock, 'but if Flack continued to ride the way he was goin', he's a dead man.'

'All Sloane has to do is line his Sharps back along his own tracks, pull the trigger when something moves,' Haggard agreed. 'He'll use what cover he can find, set tight and wait.'

Libbie Ransome spoke tremulously. 'I thought you were dead. Next time you will be. I told you once, I want no more of this.' She shook her head despairingly. 'Gade, you promised me this would be over by sunset. It can be, but only if we ride away from here, forget Diamond Jack Sloane.'

Thoughtfully, his eyes on Gade Haggard, Shako Gunn said, 'There'll be two, three hours of darkness out there.'

'Then clear moonlight,' Haggard said, nodding.

'By now Sloane'll've seen Flack from

a distance, on his own. He'll maybe figure you an' me have moved a mile or so north below these eastern slopes, intend comin' at him from that side.' He took a drink of hot coffee, sucked his teeth. 'He'll be expectin' us to move fast. We'll do that, but from the opposite direction. Circle around to the west in the darkness. Let him stew till he's half crazy jumpin' at shadows, hit him when the moon's full.'

'Me, not you,' Haggard said flatly. He flung the coffee dregs hissing into the fire, stood up. 'Everything you say makes sense — but like I said, you stay well back with Libbie.'

'And I have no say in this?' Libbie's voice shook, but now it was with anger.

'You had your say, Sis,' Gade Haggard said quietly. 'I love you, and respect your opinion. But your thinking was wrong in one important respect. In time, maybe we could do it — but Diamond Jack Sloane will never, ever forget.'

He moved to his horse, swung stiffly into the saddle, and without a backward glance rode over the ridge into the gathering gloom.

* * *

Dazed, shaken, Reuben Flack heard the flat whoomp of the big rifle and even in his confusion knew that the man who had squeezed the trigger was firing from the safety of a ridge of low rocks Flack had spotted — and recognized — more than a thousand yards ahead.

An instant before the dull detonation carried to his ears, the heavy slug had slammed into his horse's forehead. The horse stumbled, then fell like a sack of grain. Thrown clear, Flack had rolled instinctively, then wriggled like a sidewinder across the hot dust until he now lay in the shelter of his dead mount's body.

The setting sun was a rim of gold peeking over the horizon. In the dying light, the fine trickle of blood glistened wet between the horse's sightless, glassy eyes. The dead horse's bulk cast a long pale shadow. Lying in that shadow, Reuben Flack's mind drifted reluctantly back fifteen years. Long buried memories resurfaced, causing his big body to be racked by uncontrollable shudders of primitive fear.

Jack Sloane had shot with uncanny accuracy in the fading light and cooling air, placing his shot with care. All those years ago, Reuben Flack had done the same, his parched lips cracking as he laughed crazily at the blazing sun and deliberately shot the horse out from under the man who was following him across the Staked Plains.

He knew now that man was Diamond Jack Sloane's father.

Unbuckling the saddle-bag with trembling fingers, Flack dragged out his canteen, took a long swig; shuddered, spat, deliberately clenched his teeth; rolled to a sitting position against the warm body of his horse and took a deep breath.

The sun had gone. Full darkness was only minutes away. That wiped out Sloane's advantage. Under cover of that darkness Flack knew he should be able to work his way towards the low rock slabs without being seen. Once there . . .

Hell, what was at stake here? Several thousand bucks in gold pieces?

A man's honour?

Or much, much more?

A strangled laugh gurgled behind Reuben Flack's clenched teeth.

There was no honour among thieves. And a man who had once killed with cold, calculated cruelty could in return expect no quarter. So he had to get to those rocks. He had to reach them without being seen. And when he got there, by God he had to make damn sure he was in the right position to come up behind Sloane — and shoot him in the back.

Another shudder racked his heavy body. He licked dry lips, strove desperately to blank his mind to fear.

But it refused to go away. Because Flack knew that if he slipped up, in a matter of hours he would be screaming for the merciful release of death.

Diamond Jack Sloane had used the Sharps to good effect, but that would now be abandoned. Now he would rely on the sixgun and the knife. If he got his hands on Reuben Flack he would strip him naked, spreadeagle him on the plain with his wrists and ankles lashed to stakes, slice off his eyelids, and leave him to die in agony as the midday sun fried his eyeballs.

For, Reuben Flack recalled with a vividness that made him sick to his belly, on a salt flat not five miles from these same rocks, that was exactly the treatment he had meted out to Diamond Jack Sloane's father.

★ ★ ★

More than two miles to the west of where Jack Sloane casually unhorsed Reuben Flack, Gade Haggard heard the heavy bellow of the big Sharps Buffalo, in the gathering darkness clearly saw the bright muzzle flash in a low ridge of flat rock some way across the desert to the north-east.

Ten minutes later, as he rode steadily northwards, the sun's brilliant rim sank below the horizon, and quickly the Staked Plains became dark and eerily still beneath luminous skies flanked by banks of thick cloud floating high over the fertile prairie far to the east and west.

Haggard had no way of knowing if Sloane's shot had killed Reuben Flack. His gut feeling was that the gunslinger had not lured the major this far to kill him cleanly, from a distance. Sloane was still playing his cruel game. The shot was not an attempt to kill, nor was it a warning.

It was a challenge, flung down by a man confident of his prowess with a sixgun.

Here I am, Reuben Flack. If you want me, come and get me.

That being the case, Flack would be unharmed. He would now know exactly where Sloane was holed up. And for Sloane to have opened fire, and sent the slug whistling close, Flack had to be within a thousand yards of the gunman's position.

Haggard dismounted, took out his field-glasses and sank down on one knee in the warm dust. From that position, any object bigger than a pebble on the immense, flat plain, would be outlined against the night skies.

His steady riding had brought him level with the low rock ridge where he had seen the muzzle flash, but still a mile or so to the west. As soon as he focused the glasses on those rocks, he picked out Sloane's horse. Of the gunslinger, there was no sign. He would be hunkered down under cover, watching his front.

Haggard panned the glasses swiftly right, searching an area roughly three-quarters of a mile back, grunted with satisfaction as he saw an unmistakeable, rounded bulk. One purpose of the single shot was now clear: Sloane had gone for the horse, and Flack was on foot.

Then, aware that there was an object he had half seen through the moving lenses, he tracked back with the glasses and immediately located Reuben Flack. He was moving at a crouch about halfway between his dead mount and the rocks.

By swinging the glasses almost ninety degrees right, Haggard was able to locate Shako Gunn and Libbie. They were a mile further south, riding at little more than walking pace. Haggard knew that Gunn was following Sloane's tracks that were now overlaid with those of Flack's horse. If the two riders continued at that same pace, they would reach the dead horse shortly after Reuben Flack closed in on Diamond Jack Sloane.

And that was close enough, Haggard decided grimly. Gunplay was inevitable.

When the bullets began to fly, he wanted Libbie protected by Shako Gunn, and well away from the action.

He put away the field-glasses. As he fumbled for the stirrup he was suddenly almost overcome by weakness. The horizon tilted, and he was forced to grab the saddle horn and hang on while he rested his head and sucked great gulps of air through his open mouth.

Then, steadier, knowing that this, now, was the reckoning, he swung heavily into the saddle and pointed his horse towards the distant rocks.

★ ★ ★

Diamond Jack Sloane's laugh rang out of the darkness, freezing Reuben Flack where he stood.

He was out in the open, no more than twenty yards from the rocks. His fancy sixgun was in his hand, cocked. But the mocking laughter was disembodied, against the paler

245

background the outline of the low ridge smooth and unbroken.

'Watched you all the way,' Sloane called, gloating. 'Remember what I said, first time we met? You want a man to come to you, make it look easy. Hell, I could've cut you in half.'

The fool's talking too much, Flack thought, and his lips drew back in a silent snarl. Saw me from a distance, but he's forced to duck down so he lost me when I got close.

And, eyes straining, he drifted silently to his right.

Sloane's horse was a clear silhouette above the rocks. By his voice, the gunslinger was behind the rocks some way to the left of his mount.

'You're bluffing!' Flack yelled, and instantly took off in a crouching run. He scuttled crabwise to his left, then made a dart for the ridge. He was almost there when his right boot came down on a loose rock. It rolled. His ankle twisted. A bolt of agony shot up his leg. He yelped, then clamped his teeth as he toppled forward. The sixgun clattered against the rock.

Then, from behind the distant cloud banks that had delayed its rising, the bright disc of the full moon floated into clear skies. The edges of darkness were pushed back, racing across the desert as cold, clear light washed across the Staked Plains. The low ridge became sharply outlined. Sloane's horse whickered softly, turned its head, eyes glinting in the light.

And a lean black shape came leaping over the rocks, landed almost on top of Reuben Flack.

Diamond Jack Sloane hit the ground with bent legs. At point-blank range the sixgun in his right hand blasted. Hot lead whanged off the rock along-side Flack's left knee. A second shot plucked at his boot. A third seared across his thigh like a white-hot branding iron.

Wants me alive, Flack thought wildly. Wants me staked out in the sun, screaming.

Still slumped against the rock he

snapped a shot at Sloane, missed, lunged forwards. At the first step, his ankle crumpled. He roared, toppled sideways. He landed on dust-covered rock. His wrist cracked against the ground. The sixgun flew out of his hand.

Jack Sloane stepped back, grinning. His unshaven face was pale in the light of the moon. Teeth gleamed white against black stubble. His single eye glittered. He lifted the .44. There was an oily click as he thumbed back the hammer. He took careful aim at Flack's right knee.

'No, damn you!' Flack yelled. With a wide sweep of his arm he scooped up a handful of white dust and flung it into Sloane's face. In a continuation of the movement he rolled, came up clutching the sixgun.

Above him, Jack Sloane reeled backwards, pawing at his eye. Choking, spitting, he blasted a shot blind. Then he stumbled, sat down hard. The back of his head cracked against the rock.

It saved his life. On his knees, Reuben Flack loosed a shot, saw it wing its way harmlessly over Sloane's head.

And from a sitting position, eye streaming, blood trickling from his nose, spittle running down his whiskery chin, Diamond Jack Sloane coolly shot Reuben Flack through the heart.

★ ★ ★

'Don't even think about it,' Gade Haggard said.

'Well, well,' Sloane said softly. He watched the mounted figure approach, spat, dragged a sleeve across his mouth, said scornfully, 'Gade Haggard. The man from San Miguel.'

'That story's festered for too long,' Haggard said. ' 'Bout time the record was set straight.'

'You know there's only one way this can be settled.' Carefully, Jack Sloane climbed to his feet, slipped the sixgun into its holster. 'Or do you only shoot little boys.'

'I just tried to tell you — '

'Don't waste your breath.' Sloane moved away from the rocks, stepped delicately over the body of Reuben Flack. 'Climb down, or make your play from there. Either way suits me.'

'And if I turn around, ride away?'

'You get it in the back.'

Haggard sighed. He thought of the two mounted figures a thousand yards away; the blanket-draped Shako Gunn; the sister he remembered with pigtails and a freckled face, and had rediscovered as a beautiful woman. And he looked beyond Sloane, at the high bright moon, at the clouds rimmed with silver.

Then he lazily kicked his left leg over the saddle horn, dismounted the wrong side of the roan and was going for his gun before his feet had hit the ground.

Diamond Jack Sloane was fast.

Like greased lightning his gloved hand dipped. Splayed fingers touched the butt of his Dragoon. The pistol snicked out of the holster. It was blasting as it came level.

But he was not fast enough.

Or, Haggard thought later, maybe he was — but he'd been outsmarted.

Gade Haggard made his draw as he dropped. He let his knees buckle as he pulled the trigger.

The two shots blasted as one. Flaming muzzle flashes dimmed the light of the moon.

Diamond Jack Sloane's slug plucked the stetson from Gade Haggard's head.

Then Sloane's sixgun fell from suddenly nerveless fingers. He grunted, reached across to grasp his right forearm with his left hand.

Slowly, Haggard straightened. He watched the bright droplets of red blood from Sloane's arm patter into the dust; watched the gunman crouch, pick up his sixgun left handed, by its hot barrel.

'I was never in San Miguel,' Haggard said. 'I didn't shoot your son.'

Sloane shrugged. 'There's no proving

it, either way.' He jerked his thumb at Reuben Flack. 'But about him, there was no doubt.'

'No, there never was. I saw something in his eyes when he rode out of the Staked Plains. I was a kid. What I saw was murder, but all I knew was it was bad.'

'So — what about me?'

Weariness was in Gade Haggard's bones. With it there was a sudden hatred of violence, of death. He thought of Libbie's words, knew that if she could let this man walk away, so could he.

He holstered his .44, held out his hand.

'Throw me your gun. Then go. Ride out of my life — and stay out.'

For an agonizing few seconds Diamond Jack Sloane hesitated. Then he nodded curtly, tossed the gun underarm towards Gade Haggard. It spun, glinting in the moonlight, an arc of deadly steel.

It was still in the air when the slug

from Sam Pickens's Hawken plains rifle slammed into Diamond Jack Sloane's chest, ploughed through bone and muscle into his heart and drove him back against the rocks, dead.

★ ★ ★

'They're talking,' Shako Gunn said.

'And Flack's still down?'

'Down, dead — who knows.'

They were dismounted, alongside Reuben Flack's dead horse. Shako Gunn had field-glasses pressed to his eyes. Libbie Ransome was leaning across the saddle of Sam Pickens's horse, his Hawken rifle to her shoulder.

As the moonlight flooded the Staked Plains they had clearly seen Diamond Jack Sloane gun down Reuben Flack, then watched what seemed to be an unresolved blur of action as Gade Haggard slid from his horse.

'Gade's lifted his hand . . . ' Gunn said hesitantly.

Libbie pressed her cheek against the

rifle, looked across the sights; centred the foresight on Sloane's chest.

Then, through the glasses, Flack caught Diamond Jack Sloane's sudden movement, the flash of metal.

'Shoot him!' he rapped.

His words were drowned by the roar of the rifle.

In the sudden, aching silence, Libbie's breath caught in a sob.

★ ★ ★

'He was drawing on you,' she told Gade. 'Shako saw him through the glasses. He went for his gun — and I shot him.'

The bodies of Diamond Jack Sloane and Reuben Flack had been dragged so that they lay together against the rocks.

Shako Gunn was gazing down at them. He saw the bloody, useless right arm of Diamond Jack Sloane, the holster tied down to his right thigh, tried to recall what had seen through the glasses.

Then he slipped the old Indian blanket from his shoulders, and used it to cover the two bodies.

'Sure,' he said. 'I told you, the man was goin' for his gun. If you hadn't shot him . . .'

His arm around Libbie's shoulders, Gade Haggard said, 'It's over. Mount up. We're going home.'

THE END

Other titles in the
Linford Western Library:

THE BOUNTYMEN

Tom Anson

Tom Quinlan headed a bunch of other bounty hunters to bring in the long-sought Dave Cull, who was not expected to be alone. That they would face difficulties was clear, but an added complication was the attitude of Quinlan's strong-minded woman, Belle. And suddenly, mixed up in the search for Cull, was the dangerous Arn Lazarus and his men. Hunters and hunted were soon embroiled in a deadly game whose outcome none could predict.

THE EARLY LYNCHING

Mark Bannerman

Young Rice Sheridan leaves behind his adoptive Comanche parents and finds work on the Double Star Ranch. Three years later, he and his boss, Seth Early, are ambushed by outlaws, and their leader, the formidable Vince Corby, brutally murders Early. Rice survives and reaches town. Pitched into a maelstrom of deception and treachery, Rice is nevertheless determined that nothing will prevent him from taking revenge on Corby. But he faces death at every turn . . .